Ciao Mar

Death in Southwark

A medieval whodunnit

Mariella Moretti
Colin Sowden

The novel is based on real historical events and draws on surviving documents and accounts of the period. However, as it is a work of fiction, some characters, places and situations are imaginary, though plausible, and any apparent significance that might be attached to these outside the story would be purely accidental.

Preface

In Southwark, a notorious district of London, a well-known merchant dies in mysterious circumstances. In the ensuing investigation, Sarah, the merchant's young wife, is accused of the crime. She is imprisoned and, if found guilty, will be hanged.

The affair of the murder is interwoven with events surrounding Kathryn Howard, unfaithful fifth wife of King Henry VIII. As the young queen goes to the scaffold, Sarah's flight and emotional struggle also come to an unpredictable end.

Contents

"He should have died then."

"My mother called it common sense…"

A dead end

Blackmail

The astrologer doctor

A note of jealousy

"Because she's dead."

In the merchant's house

Esther Godfrey

"So young and so beautiful."

"It happened last year."

"What became of Culpepper?"

Sarah

A posthumous accusation

"There's some intrigue behind this."

Burnt alive, like a witchcraft

The Clink

Shiny, black cockroaches

"Because I don't know how to write."

"I shall be hanged for what I did."

Characters

Esther Godfrey, doctor Godfrey's sister. "It seems that she is rather a nasty piece of work. She hated that poor Tiler, and she hates Sarah."

Joseph Godfrey, astrologist doctor, father of Sarah, wife of the murdered merchant. "He is heavily built, thick lips, double chin, speaks in a voice that makes the rafters ring. Arrogant. Confides with false modesty that he is the King's favourite physician, indeed the best there is in London..."

Henry VIII (1491-1547), King of England and Lord of Ireland and the Islands. Married six times and wielding absolute power, he had a profound influence on the political and religious history of his country. In order to marry Anne Boleyn, he put away his first wife, Katharine of Aragon, who died of grief in a remote castle, and broke with the Church of Rome, giving rise to the Church of England.
"As a young man hailed as 'the handsomest prince in Christendom', he became "an obese tyrant, his face swollen, his stomach mountainous, one leg covered in sores and threatening to turn gangrenous...".

Kathryn Howard (1525-1542), fifth wife of King Henry VIII. "That day she looked beautiful in her dress of white brocade, her hair silky, the colour of copper, falling down over her shoulders as though she were a maiden, her skin clear, her eyes a luminous blue, full of love as she looked at me, then cast down in modesty."

Lady Constance, wife of the coroner Sir Robert Kytchyn, whom she supports and helps in his investigations. "She was taller than her husband, her eyes green flecked with gold, a determined nose, a resolute stance, graceful in her cream-coloured brocaded dress, with a head-dress the same flame-red colour as her hair."

Margery Ackworth, governess to Lady Constance. "It was difficult to say how old Margery was: the woman was strong, energetic, skilled at washing with cinders. She had bright cheeks in a rubicond face, with fine veins under pale-blue eyes. Only the gnarled hands and the odd grey curl which escaped from under her bonnet betrayed her real age."

Matthew Tiler, a rich old merchant, found stabbed to death in an alleyway in the docks area of London. "A man who has passed sixty, of middle height, grown thin with age, delicate. The hair grey and sparse, the skin pale. The teeth few, and in poor condition. The hands: dry as branches in winter, scarred, probably injured in a fire, the nails black, twisted, thick..."

Philip Glover, pupil and assistant to Sir Robert Kytchyn, "was a tall, slender youth, with a clear complexion, eyes the colour of light chestnut, and the carefully tended beginnings of a beard."

Sarah Tiler née Godfrey, young wife of the murdered merchant. "She was slight and graceful of figure. She had dark hair that stood out against the pale green of her dress, the neck slender, the face sad, with high cheekbones, retaining something of the child's shyness."

Sir Barnaby Lowell, son of Sir Henry Lowell of Hungerford, Gentleman of the Bedchamber to the king. "He was a tall, broad shouldered young man, the frank eyes of youth, a hint of blond beard on his chin, with the hue of someone who spends much time in the open air."

Sir Daniel Shipwith, gentleman in the service of the Lord of Carlisle. "A sturdy young man, descendant of mariners, with a hooked nose, thick chestnut eyebrows, dark eyes and a frank, jovial manner."

Sir James Wright, a ward of Sir Nicholas Sherman. "An athletic young man, with brown hair, clear blue eyes, and a gentle soul."

Sir Nicholas Sherman, gentleman in the service of the Duke of Norfolk and a friend of Sir Robert Kytchyn, whom he assists in his investigations. "He had fought with Norfolk against the Scots and acted as ambassador on several missions. He had thin lips in a bony face, a prominent nose and penetrating, deep-sunken steel-grey eyes."

Sir Robert Kytchyn, Dean of Pembroke College, Cambridge, doctor and coroner, entrusted by the King with the inquest into the death of Matthew Tiler. "He was a man of about forty, with some marks of age on his lively face, his hair already grey and always ruffled, a bulge developing around his waist, pale-blue eyes behind small horn-rimmed glasses, giving him the appearance of a wise old owl."

Thomas Howard, third Duke of Norfolk (1473-1554), uncle of two of Henry VIII's wives. Cruel and unscrupulous, he was imprisoned in the Tower following the downfall of his niece Kathryn.

Places

Southwark is a district of London to the south of London Bridge. Before Henry VIII's break with Rome, a large part of the area was covered with abbeys and monasteries, and about a third of the population comprised monks and nuns. After the schism the majority of the buildings belonging to the religious orders were seized and given over to members of the king's inner circle at court.

Although prostitutes could be found in other parts of the city, Southwark was their preferred venue because of its vicinity to the port and because the area abounded in taverns and cheap boarding houses. There they could find lodging on those occasions when, in order to curb the spread of syphilis, they were forbidden to practise their trade openly.

The Palace of Whitehall overlooked the upper stretch of the River Thames in its course through the city. When the Henry VIII's Lord Chancellor, Thomas Wolsey, fell into disgrace, the sovereign appropriated it, made lavish improvements, in the process incorporating surrounding parklands, and turned it into a new royal residence. Among the more striking were a bowling green, a tennis court and a ground for tournaments. In the chapel there Henry married two of his wives, Anna Boleyn and James Seymour, and died in the palace in 1547.

Hampton Court, that grandiose red-brick palace which rises amidst the verdant splendour of meadows and gardens a few miles from London, also belonged to Cardinal Wolsey, who had taken it as his personal residence before Henry forced him to surrender it. Legend states hat Kathryn Howard, fifth unfaithful wife of the sovereign, still wanders there weeping.

The Tower of London served over the centuries as fortress, royal abode, prison and torture chamber. William the Conqueror began the building in 1070, and in the course of time, other parts were added, each one bearing the stamp of the monarch who ordered it.

The Castle of Carlisle, in Cumberland, built in pink and grey stone, goes back to 1092, when William Rufus, third son of William the Conqueror, erected it on the heights which overlook the River Eden at this point. Since the English city of Carlisle is situated on the border with Scotland, it was often attacked by the Scots, and the castle, subjected to long sieges, was lost and recaptured on several occasions by both sides in conflict with each other.

Clink Prison
In Tudor times 'The Clink' was one of the most feared prisons in the kingdom, and the only one from that period still standing. As the oldest prison in England, it is the one with the longest and most sordid history. Now transformed into a grisly museum, it can still be found in Southwark.

The Royal Hospital of Saint Mary of Bethlehem (Bedlam)

It was the only institution in Europe specifically for the criminally insane, those accused of unusual violence or infanticide, where inmates were commonly subjected to quite deplorable treatment.

'Bedlam', a corruption of Saint Mary of Bethlehem, came to be used as an expression signifying madness, chaos, confusion.

Cripplegate

Built in 1099, Cripplegate was a gate in the London Wall, the others being Ludgate, Newgate, Aldersgate, Bishopsgate, Moorgate.

The origins of the gate's name are uncertain. One theory suggests it is named after the cripples who used to beg there. The name of the nearby medieval church of St Giles-without-Cripplegate lends credence to this suggestion as Saint Giles is the patron saint of cripples and lepers.

Prologue

London, 18 January 1542

On the night of 17 January 1542 an old merchant called Matthew Tiler was found dead in an ill-famed district of London, his throat cut open. Below is the letter that the self-confessed killer wrote a few days after the crime:

**Written in London,
The eighteenth day of January, 1542**

My dearest sister, I beseech your prayers as once again I open my heart to you in what is perhaps the most desperate moment of my life.

You will remember what I have written to you of an old merchant of Southwark, of his young wife, of my torment, because I was falling in love with this woman. Well, last night that old man was murdered, and I am the killer that all London is searching for at this moment.
When I confided to you that the woman was married to someone else, I put to you the question: 'What right has the old man to come between us if she and I love one another?'

'That woman is his wife,' you replied. And you urged me not to consider doing anything wrong. I revealed to you, then, that for some time there had been another person inside me, someone that I did not know, who had come from I knew not where, who took me into places that were foreign to me, and horrible. So, when I fell asleep, my dreams became nightmares – I pictured the old man attacked by robbers, pushed into a sack and thrown alive into the Thames, or tortured in the Tower dungeons, and that I tore out his heart with my bare hands. And in my dreams I enjoyed all this.

'And when you awoke?' you asked me.

I replied that I was shocked, and ashamed of myself. But that when day came, I again imagined how I might...

'End his life?' you ventured.

Today I can tell you that I did.

It was the night that I had decided to confront him. I was going to challenge him, to shout in his face that she did not love him, that he was a useless old man – she was still a virgin when I made her mine. That he should get out of the way, that if he didn't do so, I'd do it for him.

It was cold that night, the roofs were covered with snow, the streets frozen over, shining like mirrors. I was hiding behind the parapet which shields Thames Street from the river, watching the guests leaving Whitehall palace, a few at a time, at the end of the royal banquet. Finally, there he was. It wasn't difficult to follow him: he was taking the small steps of an old man who was afraid of slipping on the ice. If I lost sight of him when he went round a corner, the light that his lantern shed along the walls made it easy for me to find him again.

But now the man crossed through the gardens of St Mary Overy and headed into the alleyways around the port. No-one around, the taverns and brothels had already closed. There was the occasional distant voice, the neighing of a horse in a stall...

And as he turned the corner of St Michael's Alley, I came alongside him. I wanted to unleash on him the evil creature inside me, like a mad dog. But he did not give me the chance. When I called out his name, he turned round. He put down the lantern, approached me and put a hand on my shoulder: in the dark I thought that he was about to pull out a dagger, so I seized mine and held it to his throat. He is shorter than me, and frail. He said 'What do you want of me, my friend?'

I was taken aback: the man that I detested, who perhaps knew about his wife and me, called me his friend! It was so unexpected. How often had I imagined that moment, with a different outcome. Because instead of confronting me, he suddenly started gasping, as if he couldn't breathe. He raised a hand to his chest, staggered forward, and fell on top of me. Instinctively I tried to stop him falling, but he slid to the ground like a bunch of rags, without a sound. Perhaps he hit his head against a step: he did not move again. He lay there, limp, his cap just beyond, his hair grey. I bent down and felt his throat: he was dead.

Now a clear moon came out from behind the clouds and illuminated the alleyway. Only then did I see that my dagger had pierced his throat, only then did I feel my hand hot and sticky. I had killed him.

Dear sister, yes, I had killed him, and I couldn't come to terms with what had happened. One voice inside me was saying 'In fact, isn't this what you wanted?' Another one accused me: 'You're a murderer!'

My heart seemed to be bursting out of my chest, I felt suddenly faint. And in a little while the watch would be making their round, and they would find me with a dead man on my hands.

What was I to do? My own cold-bloodedness astonished me. I knelt down and removed the gold guild chain from around his neck and the money bag from his belt: a robber has killed him, they would think. I didn't dare to take off his gloves and remove his rings – I had learned in Southwark that he had burnt his hands horribly in a mysterious fire.
I looked at him again: his eyes were open, staring at me, his face thin and marked with fine wrinkles: he reminded me of our father on the morning he died.
A cold wind, unexpectedly. 'He will be cold too,' I found myself thinking. The lantern was nearly out. I put the cap back on his head and pulled his cloak over him. And why did I suddenly feel pity? Why were my eyes filling with tears?"

The light of the lantern was failing. I found myself leaving the alleyway, and knocking on the shutters of a nearby inn called the Tabard. A small window above the door opened and there appeared a young woman, a prostitute, Agnes. She recognized me, came down and opened the door – she is a good country girl, affectionate. I had often been with her, even though my heart was elsewhere. She asked me nothing: as I collapsed on the bench, she placed a tankard of beer on the grate, and when it was warm she gave it to me to drink. She comforted me by saying nothing She had some clothes of mine that I had left there for her to mend. She helped me to tidy myself and get changed, put on different boots.

It was still dark when I left Southwark. As I crossed London Bridge I threw the money and the gold chain into the river below.

But today I have found out that the old merchant's wife, the woman that I love...

The letter of the alleged murderer, discovered in Ireland many years later among his sister's papers, broke off here.

The morning after

London, Southwark

It was not yet dawn – a reluctant winter dawn – when there was a knock at the door of Sir Robert Kytchyn. At that time the coroner was in London at the Chancery Court for a case regarding a goldsmith, whom it was suspected had been poisoned.

Sir Robert was now about fifty, the hair grey, curly, bunched around the beginnings of a bald patch on his crown, and the drooping shoulders of one who spent many hours over books. He retained the pale-blue eyes of his youth, together with the crafty look of the villagers from amongst whom he had sprung. "My family was so poor," he would sometimes say, "that my father often risked the gallows for poaching in the king's forests, and my mother had hands and knees ruined by years of washing clothes in the stream." This had left him with a shade of diffidence, above all when in the company of gentlemen used to the ease conferred by generations of authority and wealth.

When Robert was ten years old, the rector of the catechism school had spoken about him to the Dean of Pembroke College in Cambridge. The latter had taken him as a pupil.

Year by year the boy had grown to be a cultured young man, then an expert doctor, eventually a figure of such authority in the field of pathology that he had been invited to teach at that University, and had been knighted by King Henry VIII – a title that he never flaunted.

The knocking at the door eventually woke him. Recognizing the voice of his friend Sir Nicholas Sherman, the doctor threw a blanket over his shoulders and went to pull back the bolt.

"Dress quickly," said Sir Nicholas. "One of the king's confidants has been killed this night. The king has charged you with the investigation, you are to act as his personal coroner."

"My God, not again!" groaned Sir Robert. Six years previously the king had asked him to lead an inquiry which had involved his second wife, Anne Boleyn, whose life had ended on the scaffold. The memory of those sanguinary days still haunted him.

"Don't' you remember?" said Sir Robert. "It was six years ago, King Henry had charged me with and investigation which involved Anne Boleyn, his second wife.

"I recall it. The trial? A farce for freeing himself of her. And the outcome, the scaffold."

"Those bloody days still haunt me," murmured Sir Robert. He brought his hand to his head: "And then, haven't you noticed? My hair has become grey since then, I'm almost an old man."

He turned to his friend with a pleading look, which was ignored.

So he poured some water from a jug into a small bowl and washed his hands and face. The room was bare, the fire in the grate now spent, the water freezing. The inn, the White Stag, was not for people of his rank, but he chose to lodge there because it was near the court, and because he was frugal in spending the money of which he now had ample.

He dressed rapidly. Soon after the two men descended a creaking wooden staircase, in the courtyard an attendant was holding the halters of two horses which had already been saddled. Sir Robert stroked the muzzle of his mount, smelt the odour of the gentle beast: "Asklepios, my old friend, so they have pulled you from your bed too..."
Sir James Wright, a ward of Sir Nicholas, was waiting for them together with some guardsmen. A tall young man with brown hair, clear blue eyes and a gentle soul. He and the soldiers were stamping their feet on the ground to try and warm them.
They mounted, and the party headed at a brisk trot towards the south bank of the Thames.
"Who has been killed?" Sir Robert asked his friend.
"A merchant, Mathew Tiler. He comes from a family of builders, in Staffordshire, I believe. They have grown rich from making tiles. Officially Tiler supplied King Henry with building materials for his residences: Hampton Court, Richmond, Greenwich. In fact, though, he travelled the breadth of the kingdom, gathering information useful to the crown."
"A spy?"
"In these difficult times a valuable informer, one of the few trusted confidants which the king had left. Rich now. Despite that, he continued to live in the old docks area, without pretensions. When he was killed, last night, he was indeed returning home after a banquet at court. Without escort, because he was known and well-liked by all."

Sir Robert and Sir Nicholas had become acquainted at Cambridge, during their years of study there. Sherman too had been born in a village near Cambridge, and had entered Queen's College on a scholarship. Reserved by nature, he had thin lips in a bony face, with a prominent nose and penetrating, deep-sunken steel-grey eyes. He was sturdier than Robert, and at least two spans taller. To the extent that he had often defended the other against the provocations of the older students. Once, when one of these was about to start hitting the then-skinny Robert, he had grabbed him by the scruff of the neck and hurled him out of the window onto the rose-bed below.

Then the paths of the two had diverged: Nicholas had left Cambridge, had entered the court in London and had fought with the Duke of Norfolk against the Scots. Testament to this was the scar which crossed his chin, livid, where his beard did not grow. Over the years his frame had grown even more massive, and his face had become severe.

'Has his heart perhaps hardened too?' wondered Sir Robert that first evening, when they had met again during the reception at the royal palace of Whitehall: it was known that Norfolk's orders in war were pitiless – no prisoners to be taken, the rebels to be hung from the doors of their houses, or in the country to be suspended from trees, where they were left to rot, and too bad for them if they were women or helpless old men.

Fear, perhaps, not grief

London, Southwark

While Sir Robert, Sir Nicholas, Sir James and the guards made their way towards the docks, the city awakened. Some artisans were opening the shutters of their workshops, some women were emptying chamber pots out of windows, attentive to which way the wind was blowing.

They crossed London Bridge in a line, and the light from their torches reflected off the still-dark waters of the Thames. Beyond the bridge, facing the fronts of old palaces which bordered the river, appeared Southwark, that suburb of poor dilapidated houses, with their sloping roofs so close to each other that even at midday the sunlight struggled to reach the alleyways below. Walls with peeling plaster, blue and green doorways where the varnish had cracked, horse droppings, rancid kitchen waste. Later that day, grimy little pigs would issue from some of those doors to fight over the refuse with seagulls coming from the river.

Entering these squalid lanes, the three gentlemen and their escort arrived in St Michael's Alley. The merchant's body was huddled against the steps of a baker's shop. Around were footmarks, bloodstains on the snow, and royal troops who, later, would keep the curious away. A friar in a grey habit, sandalled feet blue with cold, was kneeling beside the corpse: with closed eyes and clasped hands, his lips moving in silent prayer.

All dismounted. Sir Nicholas gestured to a guard to keep hold of their horses. Sir Robert removed from under his saddle a blanket which he draped over his old horse's back to keep him warm. Then crouched beside the body, felt the artery on the neck with two fingers, gently closed the man's eyes. Even after years of medical practice he was moved by the thought of how much more there was beyond the mere corpse: the feelings, the hopes, the memories.

"Strange," observed Sir Nicholas, standing next to him. "His cap stayed on his head when he fell."

Sir Robert carefully turned the dead man's head to one side: "No, it was placed there afterwards. Do you see? The cranium is in a bad state, there is dirt in the hair."

"And so?"

"If the cap had stayed on his head when he fell, the dirt would be on the cap, not in his hair. So it was placed there. I wonder why."

He added: "Did you notice? The face is peaceful, as if he had been talking to a friend. Someone whom he didn't fear."

"Which means?"

Sir Robert smiled at him: "Nicholas, I'll let you into a little secret. This is what investigators call a clue," he said, not without a hint of irony, as if wishing to tease his friend.

The cap on the head and the calm expression: Sir Robert was already wondering where those clues might lead.

The dead man's cloak was of a costly dark green velvet, lined with fur. Sir Robert moved it aside, saw the slit throat,

the shirt soaked in blood, a dagger on the ground nearby —
a Florentine stiletto with an engraved silver hilt.

"He is not wearing his gold guild chain, and there is no
money in the purse at his belt," he remarked.

"So the killer is a thief," responded Sir Nicholas.

"Who leaves behind a precious dagger? Unlikely." Sir
Robert smiled. "Which gives us an advantage, however. If
we had been sure that this was the work of a thief, we
would have had to search among the hundreds of
vagabonds that crowd the city. But the abandoned dagger
suggests that we must look elsewhere."

"Which means?"

"Almost certainly the killer removed the chain and the
money in order to feign a robbery, but in fact the nature of
the crime is rather different."

Sir Robert rose and saw Sir James, the king's young
gentleman who had accompanied them, vomiting, one hand
against the wall.

"The dead man and the boy knew each other?" asked Sir
Nicholas.

"Both frequented the court. Perhaps Sir James drank too
much at the king's banquet last night."

"Or perhaps his stomach is too young to stand such a sight
as this."

He approached him and put a hand on his shoulder. "Go
back to Whitehall, lad. And you, Nicholas, send word
around your informers. I must know in what circles the old
man moved, who his friends were, if he had enemies. And
give orders to trace the chain, in the taverns and at the
bottom of the river. Promise a reward in coin to whoever
can provide information."

"Excellent!"

Just at that moment a group of women slowly arrived:
sailors' wives with weary faces, and an old haggard-looking

prostitute, with a faded scar of the branding-iron on her cheek. Among these women a younger one stood out, wearing a white dress under a dark cloak, long black hair hanging loose, accompanied by an old woman, perhaps her governess. Although pale, the young woman had eyes as bright and black as those of a crow, and a restless air, like a gypsy.

"It's the old man's wife," explained Sir Nicholas, and gave orders to the guards to let her through. Sir Robert hurriedly covered the wound and dagger with the dead man's cloak, leaving just the face exposed. He brought her to him, guiding her by the elbow. "Do you recognize him?" he asked.

She bent down slightly to look. Then in a flat voice, "It's him. He was still alive yesterday."

"Be brave." Sir Robert looked in her eyes and seemed to read there distress: fear perhaps, but not grief.

The woman moved away and Sir Nicholas gave orders that the merchant's body be taken to a cellar at Whitehall Palace, so that Sir Robert could later conduct a *post mortem* examination.

"Put him somewhere cold," recommended the latter, "and cover him with snow."

Potions and simple herbs

London, Southwark

Having left Southwark, Sir Robert chose to head back to the Palace of Whitehall on foot. He was accompanied by Sir Nicholas, whom the King had ordered to assist him in the investigation.

"Nicholas, these are the gates that the merchant came out of alive. To return home, to his young wife," said Sir Robert. "So, tell me about her."

"The dead man's wife? Her name is Sarah. She's the daughter of Joseph Godfrey, the medical astrologist who looks after the King. The only one who's able to bring him any relief for the ulcers on his leg."

"How does he manage that?"

"While the Court doctors cauterize the sores with hot irons, and apply leeches and ground pearls – you could hear him screaming from the pain -, Godfrey uses potions and ointments made from simple herbs. You know them: yarrow, valerian, dill, vitex... Some he grows in his garden, and it appears that the daughter collects the wild ones from the wood at night, when there's a full moon."

Although the soldiers were several steps behind them, Sir Nicholas lowered his voice, leaning towards his friend: "Do you remember? Thirty years ago they were calling Henry VIII Tudor 'the virtuous ruler, the handsomest prince in Christendom'. Today, at fifty years of age and on his fifth wife, he's a degenerate old man, fat and malevolent."

Sir Robert also spoke in whispers: "It was said that his sores were a curse laid on him by Queen Anne Boleyn, 'the witch'. But from what I hear, even when he'd sent her to her death, he didn't get any better."

"Indeed, he got worse. His veins split open, his flesh seemed to be rotting, it was almost unbearable to be near him when Godfrey removed the bandages. By the way, he'll summon you in the next few days to see how your enquiries are proceeding. Be careful."

"Why so? The fact that he's trusted me with this case shows that he respects me."

"He's not reasonable any more. Beware of him. Over the years he's become savage. Like a lion in a cage, at any moment he can tear to pieces whoever is around him."

While they were walking, holding the horses by the halter, Sir Robert gazed at the city, which after Southwark appeared charming: the grand houses in white stone from Caen and pink from Burgundy gleamed in the first rays of a feeble sun, the Thames filled with boats and coloured barges, the streets grown noisy with people, horses, carts.

'And yet, the assassin that I'm condemned to find is walking these streets, among these people,' anguished Sir Robert. "Tell me, Nicholas: the daughter of that doctor, Godfrey – Sarah, I seem to remember – , has she any enemies?"

"I would not have thought so, even though the Godfreys come from Spain, and foreigners are not regarded kindly here. Sarah's mother died of fever after giving birth. Sarah was raised by her father and his sister, together with everyone in the neighbourhood. You have seen her: young, attractive with a kind of wild beauty, and she cares for the poor without asking for payment."

"The father, then, what sort of man is he?"

"Intelligent, it is said, but greedy. He knew that the king was fond of the old merchant, so when the girl had turned fifteen, he forced her to marry him, and in this way gained entry to the court. She assists him when he treats the king. She is the same age as Kathryn Howard, Henry's fifth wife, and it is said that she became her friend."

He looked behind him again and added: "Now that Kathryn is in disgrace with the sovereign, this does not work in her favour: but of that I shall tell you more later."

While the party of men re-entered Whitehall Palace through the river gate, the winter wind shook the branches of the trees along Thames Street, sending down a light shower of snow.

"My heart is with you."

London, Palace of Whitehall

Seated at a table in the rooms that had been reserved for him at Whitehall, Sir Robert wrote a letter to his wife, Lady Constance. He imagined her in their family home in Cambridge, busy with household tasks – cheerful, capable, refined. How often her feminine intuition had aided him in his enquiries. And how, over the years, had she maintained that lively spirit which had attracted him, a retiring sort of man, at their first meeting at the court in London.

The goose quill ran quickly over the straw-coloured parchment, in the silence could be heard the faint scratching.

Written from London, Whitehall
The twentieth day of January of the year 1542

My most beloved lady and spouse, I wish you peace and health and commend myself to you in my most hearty manner.

A household servant of Sir Nicholas, the friend whom I am sure you recall, will come to Cambridge with this letter and the ring that I wear on my little finger, as proof for you. Briefly: since I am obliged to remain in London longer than expected, I ask that you would join me here as soon as possible. And this not just from the affection that I have for you, that makes dismal every separation, but also because I stand in urgent need of your counsel.

I will have my pupil, Philip, accompany you. I know that it will be painful for him to return to those places that witnessed the dramatic scenes of his first love. But we have need of him here.

Of help too will be your governess Margery. She will surely complain that London is a dirty, sinister place, swarming with prostitutes and cut-throats, that one can starve to death before anyone will throw you a crust of bread, that there is a thief at every corner ready to rob you. However shall I be able to tell her that I am investigating the death of an old man found in an alley with a stab wound in his neck? For now say nothing of the affair.

And since the sovereign will soon demand an audience of me, I shall need suitable attire: have the goodness to bring this with you.

Sir Nicholas has reserved for us comfortable rooms in the superb royal palace of Whitehall. They will delight you: Arras tapestries on the walls, high arched ceilings, on the floors fresh sprigs which exude the sweet smell of meadows, windows which overlook the gardens, now covered in snow. I suppose that in the stables here they are treating my aged Asklepios with the same care that they show to the horses of the court: can you imagine the airs he

will give himself when he returns to his humble abode in
Cambridge?
My lady, even though we are far apart I am with you,
because my heart is with you."
I await you.

Yours for ever, Robert

Sir Robert dried the ink with a dusting of fine sand, shook
away the excess and folded the sheet in three. He held the
stick of wax near the candle flame, let a little fall onto the
fold and sealed it with his signet. With a few swift changes
of horse at the inns, the messenger would arrive at their
Cambridge house very early the next day.

That evening there was no entertainment at court and Sir
Robert was dining with Sir Nicholas in the latter's rooms.
The dishes came from the King's kitchens, which were
some distance away, and a servant re-heated them over a
brazier. Nevertheless, the spit-roasted meat and the stewed
fish, flavoured with herbs and spicy sauces, were
sumptuous, and the wine from the King's cellars was
delicious.
"When I think of how as a child I used to go to the door of
the lord of the manor to beg for leftovers from his table,"
recalled Sir Robert. "There was a good number of us, all in
a line, each with his bowl. The cook knew my mother,
knew that she was a good woman and sought to fish out
for me more meat than broth."
"Our families were poor too, but at least the lord of the
manor let us hunt and fish enough for us to eat," rejoined
Sir Nicholas.

"Not so in our village. Once, on the way home from my begging, I tripped and fell over. We lived in a one-room cottage, the hearth in the middle of the floor, with a hole in the thatch above to let out the smoke, and we didn't even keep a hen or a goat. When she saw me holding the fragments of the pot and what remained of the food, my mother started to cry – we didn't have another bowl."

Sir Robert sighed. "Come, let us turn to our enquiry. Nicholas, the fact that the merchant was a king's agent raises various possibilities. I wonder if we might be dealing with a conspiracy of Spanish Catholics. Or perhaps retaliation against the king by Catholics here? Or was it a matter of revenge on the part of a rival or envy on the part of a courtier? The work of a madman? Who would stand to gain by his death?"

He sighed again: "Above all, the key of this crime is in the motive. I beg you, I must know more about him."

"I often used to meet him at court," said Sir Nicholas, "he liked to talk with me. He had come to know Henry thirty years before, when the young sovereign started to restore his palaces. At the start he supplied the new monarch with bricks and lime."

"And thus he made his fortune."

"He was an honest man, the sovereign trusted him. He had learnt to write, spoke French and Flemish, travelled in those countries. It had not gone to his head, as I told you he was still living in his old house by the docks, with his young wife Sarah."

"The doctor's daughter."

"Joseph Godfrey, yes. He too lives in Southwark, with a sister. Esther by name, and old, she is about the same age as the merchant, I believe."

One question tormented Sir Robert: "Nicholas, that abandoned dagger, I wonder. I realize that one may kill for money, out of hunger, but that was not a petty thief's knife. So, why? If we can shed some light on this question, we might be able to put our hands on the killer."

Sir Nicholas went to the window. The sunset had turned to night, a moon had unexpectedly appeared and illumined all one side of the palace courtyard.

Sir Robert too rose from the table: he was not used to drinking and his head was spinning. All of a sudden he remembered something: "How is that young man who accompanied us that morning in Southwark? Is he better?"

"Sir James? He will leave soon for the North with the soldiers of the Duke of Norfolk: the Scots have again crossed the frontier. He'll be going with his old friend Sir Barnaby Lowell. Both of them are from the Berkshire gentry. Their fathers were two of King Henry's Gentlemen of the Privy Chamber, his drinking and hunting companions when they were young. In memory of their fathers, the king wants to make good soldiers of the sons, which is why he has entrusted them to me."

"He was shocked by the sight of the body, that morning."

"One must become hardened to such."

"We must all become so. As they say: it may be in the evening, it may be in the morning, but the grim reaper will not miss his appointment."

The two men parted early: the investigation the next day would be tiring. And, though they did not yet know it, full of unexpected events.

"His light is spent."

London, the cellars of Whitehall

The *post-mortem* examination took place where the merchant's body had been laid, in the cellars below the Palace of Whitehall. Sir Nicholas, Sir Robert and a secretary of Sir Nicholas made their way down along passageways dimly lit by the occasional torch on the walls. The air was dusty, there were enormous piles of firewood, wicker chests which had contained bows and arrows, joiners' tools on top of a workbench, stools with legs missing, milk churns, cases of plates in fine but unmatched porcelain. In a kind of alcove a watchman indicated a basket which spilled over with snow.

Two guards grasped the body by the armpits and ankles, laid it on a trestle table and lit more torches. Not without a struggle they removed the clothing: the cloak, the padded tunic, the breeches, the thick woollen stockings, the dark green velvet cap decorated with an expensive agatha brooch, the gloves of soft chamois leather, like the boots.

Sir Robert and Sir Nicholas covered their faces with white cloths, which they knotted at the back of their necks. They approached the table. In accordance with custom, Sir

Robert made the sign of the cross and pronounced the set formula: 'We are required to examine these poor mortal remains, may God help us.' He gestured to the secretary, who took notes.

He leant over the corpse: "Here we have a man over sixty, of middle height, grown thin with age. The hair is grey and sparse, the skin pale. Death has softened the features."

He turned the head to one side: "He has a shallow wound on his cranium, two inches long, not made with a sharp blade. There are clots of blood in his hair, mixed with dirt."

He raised his eyes towards Sir Nicholas: "I recall that he was on his back on a step clear of snow."

"It was the entrance to a baker's; it was the baker who raised the alarm well before dawn when he arrived with his apprentice to light the ovens."

Sir Robert continued: "The mouth is open, as if at the moment of death he was speaking to someone, or was gasping for air. Few teeth, and in poor condition. A deep cut in the neck, clearly made by the point of the dagger. And again I wonder, as on the other night: why did the killer not keep hold of the weapon?"

"Perhaps someone appeared, and he had to escape."

Sir Robert shook his head: "Yet he had time to remove the chain and money. And look at the hands: withered like twigs in winter, injured, probably burnt in a fire, the nails black, twisted, thick. Precious rings on the fingers – we shall give them to the widow. But why take the chain and not the rings, which were just as valuable?"

Sir Nicholas was not a patient man: "So, can you say how he died? A blow to the head? A cut throat?"

Still bending over the body, Sir Robert replied: "You see, Nicholas: we know that one can die by homicide, by suicide, accidentally, naturally..."

"And so?"

"I would rule out suicide: the man was a friend of the king's. He had a wife whom he loved, I heard whispers from the women that he was religious and charitable towards the poor."

"Accidental death, hitting his head?"

"And when dead he put his cap back on?"

"Homicide, then?"

"It is the most likely hypothesis. Even if..."

Still bent over the body, Sir Robert looked up calmly: "The type of wound and the bleeding – little blood, so the heart was no longer beating – suggest that he might not have died from the stabbing. Perhaps the shock of an assault made his heart fail. But who can say? His light is spent before time, that is all. May God grant him peace."

The burial of the merchant took place the following day in the churchyard surrounding St Mary Overy, beyond the river, just behind his house. The King sent Sir Nicholas to represent him, and Sir Robert, hidden behind the others, chose to be there too. Out of piety, out of compassion for the old man. Also because the killer might have been there, drawn, as is often the case, to those places near which the crime was committed.

The body, wrapped in a grey linen shroud, was lowered into the grave, and there were some prayers. "Adieu, Matthew Tiler, adieu poor old fellow," murmured Sir Robert. "Sit tibi terra levis."

But it was snowing heavily and when the Lord Mayor and the other dignitaries, wrapped in their scarlet cloaks, had left, there remained standing next to the mound which was rapidly becoming covered in snow, only a few women and the young widow. The latter kept looking around as if searching for someone, and when her glance rested on Sir

Robert, he noticed in her eyes the same uneasiness that he had observed on the dawn of the previous day.

Money is anonymous

London, Whitehall

As his wife had still not arrived from Cambridge, that evening too Sir Robert dined in Sir Nicholas' rooms.

"A tough case, Nicholas. Nowhere do I see light, it's all dark and foggy. There's a corpse, but no motive. He is respected by all, happy with his young wife and enjoying the king's favour. And it is not a matter of theft."

"Well, I'm combing the docks, two fishermen found the chain and purse – in the river, stuck right under the main bridge. The safe conduct pass that Tiler was carrying with him for the curfew was found further downstream, washed up on the embankment by the tide. What that means I'll leave for you to say."

"It means that the murderer is not a thief by trade, and disposing of such a pass is not easy: so he threw it in the river. A hired killer, perhaps, who might have been in trouble if found with it on him."

"But why throw away the money? Money is anonymous."

"To spurn anything to do with the dead man. Someone who had known him in the past? A servant who had sought revenge? Someone who had some link with him?"

"And the question of the rings, why not take them away with the money and the chain?"

Sir Robert reflected for a few moments, passing his fingers through his hair, a habit he had when perplexed: "That is odd," he said, "and the oddness could be a useful clue."

"How?"

"Everything which deviates from the usual should make us think. Knowing more about the victim would help us understand. If only I had known him. If I could meet one of his friends."

"And how could you?" replied Sir Nicholas.

"By returning to Southwark, perhaps mixing with the people in the quarter. Seeking to put myself in the old man's shoes: what he did in the streets that he frequented, what he thought. Strolling along the lanes, stopping to drink a beer in a tavern, getting people to talk."

"You would not be able to. The people there have other concerns: a roof over their heads, enough food to eat, logs for the fire in winter. And you are an outsider, not one of them."

He added: "They would take you for one of the king's spies, you might be risking your life." He gestured in irritation: "You're wasting time, and that alarms me."

"I'm searching for a killer, not wasting..."

Sir Nicholas interrupted him with a gesture of impatience: "You don't know how the king has changed, from what he was to how he has become: his sudden outbursts of temper, his vicious spite. If things drag on too long, he will hold me to account, not just you."

He went to a shelf where were stored several rolled parchments, tied with red ribbons, took from there a paper which was folded in four and handed it to Sir Robert: "I have made a list of all those at court who could in some way be involved in this affair. Only conjecture. The names of those who might have left Whitehall after the royal banquet and before the gates closed for the night."

"They stay closed all night?"

"Until dawn, when carts from the country start arriving with provisions."

"So anyone who lives in the palace is immediately excluded, whilst anyone who left is necessarily a suspect..."

"Let's see." Sir Robert began to read: "The following left Whitehall: Matthew Tiler, the merchant..."

"The victim."

"...and Sir James Wright, the young gentleman that I met this morning."

"He had left in the afternoon, and the captain of the guard reported that he had not seen him re-enter. But he may have been mistaken. Besides, James came to the court as a child, he's a good lad, surely above suspicion."

"Nicholas, learn this: when one is conducting an investigation, one must suspect even one's own mother."

Sir Robert's eyes had a wicked gleam, which did not come only from the king's good wine.

He continued to scan the list: "Let us see the others: Joseph Godfrey, the doctor, his daughter Sarah, his sister Esther – all the old man's family, in fact. Some washerwomen and servants with family near the docks. Two of the cooks. Then Thomas Howard, third Duke of Norfolk and his mistress."

"Elizabeth Holland."

"Yes, and an aunt of Queen Kathryn's, the dowager duchess Agnes Howard, who returned to her house in Lambeth. Lady Jane Rochford, the widow of George Boleyn, if I am not mistaken."

"And now lady-in-waiting to Queen Kathryn. It may be that she is already a prisoner in the Tower."

"On what grounds?"

"Abetting the queen, so high treason."

"A sad story. And Queen Kathryn, where is she at the moment?"

"Shut away in an abbey in Middlesex, Syon Abbey, I believe. Waiting for Parliament to decide her fate for having betrayed the king: she faces the prospect of either the scaffold or a slow death in one of the Tower dungeons. Although, as you can imagine, the sentence has already been decided."

"She is so young, I know that she is not yet eighteen."

"But she knew what she was doing."

At that moment a guard brought in a young boy, one of the many petty thieves looking for some stranger to pilfer from, and who was yelling that he had to speak to Sir Robert immediately.

The dead man in the tavern

London, Southwark, the Tabard Inn

The little street urchin formed part of a tiny network of spies that reported to Sir Robert every possible clue which might be connected with the killing of the merchant. Mere skin and bone, the urchin had a thin, cunning little face, he covered himself with shreds of clothing to keep out the cold, and there was an unpleasant smell about him. He was called Skinny, barebones: a proper name he never remembered having.

"Leave him, everything's all right," said Sir Robert, and he stroked his head.

"There's a dead man at the Tabard who looks as if he's been stabbed with a dagger, sir," said the urchin all in one breath. He grabbed a sweetmeat off the table, and held open his hand for the promised reward.

"Oh, no, my dear: no money until I know that it's worth it. And this time you come along with me," returned Sir Robert.

They left together, and Sir Robert seated him in front on his own horse, which made the boy proud and happy.

The Tabard, the best-known inn in Southwark, was situated where the road forks for Dover and Canterbury. It was there that pilgrims stayed on their way to the shrine of the St Thomas Becket in Canterbury Cathedral.

And at the Tabard there was indeed a dead man: stretched out on the ground beside a long table, he lay in a pool of blood with eyes fixed open in an expression of terror. Sir Robert crouched next to him, closed the eyes as a gesture of respect, moved aside the cloak in order to examine the wound: "He wasn't killed with a dagger, Skinny: this is a knife wound, an ordinary kitchen-knife. Do you see here? The large vein at this neck has been slit.."

"But you'll give me the money all the same?"

Sir Robert handed him a couple of coins.

"See, he was a rich man: a velvet cloak lined with fur, the cap the same colour blue as the cloak. And the boots..."

"I think they're chamois," Skinny interrupted him. "Can't I have them?"

"There will be an inquiry. Do you want to find yourself in trouble?"

"If I was as rich as that, I'd go into a tavern and have myself a whole roast piglet."

'Skin and bones, and such a well of hunger,' thought Sir Robert, and gave him a couple more coins: "Now, be on your way, the inn-keeper is coming."

The owner, a certain Thomas Master, approached Sir Robert: "A fine mess this! I'll have all the king's guards on my back, and when they get involved..."

"Do you know who he was? Did you know him?"

"I'd have noticed, clothes like that."

"There's a purse on his belt, but, look, it has been cut in half and there is no money inside."

"So the killer was a thief..."

'One of the many in this city,' thought Sir Robert. But what was he doing here, this stranger, with all the appearance of gentleman? Who could he have been? Perhaps one of the king's spies? An emissary from the pope?'

What might have been a lead, instead proved to be a mystery.

He decided that he would let loose his little spies again, that they might continue searching. For the moment, disappointed, disheartened, he mounted his horse and returned to Westminster Palace.

Lady Constance

London, Cripplegate

A messenger announced that having left Cambridge, Sir Robert's small household – his wife Lady Constance, her former governess Margery Ackworth, the pupil and assistant Philip Glover and several servants – , were nearing London.

"I shall accompany you to meet your consort, just in case you lose your way," teased Sir Nicholas, and so the two friends, escorted by some guards, headed towards Cripplegate, one of the northern entrances into the city.

The borough of Cripplegate, a meeting place for vagabonds, beggars and the lame, was unsafe even in daylight: now that evening was approaching, at the sight of these famished faces, Sir Robert was grateful to Sir Nicholas for the escort. Outside the city walls a line of lepers with their bandaged stumps hobbled towards the leper-house established by Queen Matilda, the bells tied to what remained of their arms and legs tinkling as they moved.

As soon as he saw lady Constance, Sir Robert spurred forward his horse. The animals recognizing each other, whinnied loudly. The coroner's old mount, the elderly Asklepios, took the liberty of rubbing its muzzle against that of Blanche, Lady Constance's genteel mare. Sir Robert aided his spouse to dismount, grasping her round the waist, clasped her hands in his and brought them to his lips: "Connie," he murmured, "you are as welcome as the dawn light."

She threw her arms around his neck and kissed him warmly on the mouth: "In trouble again, my love?" she whispered to him, but with such passion that the others could not help but hear, and smile.

Lady Constance was taller by a span than her husband, and younger by at least ten years. She had sparkling green eyes flecked with gold, a strong nose, a lively voice, a head of rich red hair and striking freckles. She was about twenty years old when she entered the court in London, maid-of-honour to good Queen Katherine of Aragon, the king's first wife. Intelligent and vivacious, she had been courted by numerous gentlemen, but she fell in love with a scholar from Cambridge, Sir Robert Kytchyn, in fact.

Their meeting had occurred at the king's table on Kytchyn's first consultation at court. At the great banquet, in the presence of the royal couple, Constance had found herself sitting next to him. "Everyone talking and enjoying themselves," she recounted later to any who asked her how they had met, "and Sir Robert, silent, did nothing but stare at me, and when I returned his gaze, looked down. After dinner the dancing began – I can still remember the stately pavanes, the boisterous galliards, the handsome courtiers. But he did not know how to dance, and remained looking at me fixedly. He said little all evening. The following day we happened to meet in the Whitehall gardens, he took my hand: 'My lady, I sincerely believe that we should marry,' he said. And after a few months we were in Cambridge, man and wife..."

So Constance bade farewell to a future as a lady of the manor, and to her own rich family, which opposed the marriage. She became the spouse of one of the many masters at the old university, put aside her lute and songs of courtly love and learnt to cook bread, brew beer, skim milk to make butter and cream; to make preserves and pickles, candles and soap; to weave and to sew, and to ensure for her husband a scholar's ordered life.

As for children, one had arrived immediately: a lovely strong boy, who had filled the house with his cries and his sweetness. But, born in January, he was taken by a fever in June. They had not had others: she had come close to losing her mind. The good Margery had hid her own tears, the wet nurse had been sent back to her village of Chesterton, the nursery distressingly empty. Their life's tragedy, an open wound that only those who have lost a child can know. Something of which they never spoke, out of compassion for each other, out of reticence perhaps, but which cast a shadow over their days.

Philip Glover

London, Palace of Whitehall

The arrival of Lady Constance at court was celebrated with a dinner in the great hall at Whitehall. Seated at the high table were the Duke of Norfolk representing the sovereign, the Bishop of Winchester Stephen Gardiner, and Sir Robert and his spouse. The arrangement of the trestle tables in horse-shoe fashion allowed everyone to enjoy the entertainment which had been devised in the central space: jesters, jugglers, musicians, tumblers. Later, with the tables removed, there would follow the dancing.

So the atmosphere was festive, all were enjoying themselves, and it was the bishop himself who asked Sir Robert: "That young man down next to Sir Nicholas – I have seen him with you before – , does not seem to be in good spirits at all."

"Philip? Philip Glover – he has been studying with me to become a doctor, now he acts as my secretary. He is a likeable fellow, but this place reminds him of unhappy events which happened here, in London."

"Tell me, if you may," prompted he prelate.

"It is no secret. It was six years ago, we were here to investigate who had murdered a certain William Crooks, one of the king's spies, a vile individual. At the time there was a delightful young lady at court called Alice – Lady Alice Winter of Broughton Abbey, in Leicestershire. She was maid-of-honour to Queen Anne Boleyn, and under her particular care as she was an orphan and blind.

Sir Robert gave a piece of roast meat to a dog which had rested its head on his knee and was regarding him with doleful eyes.

He continued: "The young Philip fell in love with her, and she with him. We all thought that they might marry, and be happy. But we did not realize that it was she who had killed Crooks. Crooks had tried to ensnare her, had made lewd suggestions. One day, when he was on the point of raping her, she took a candlestick and struck him on the head. She was blind, but taller than him, and smashed his skull."

"What happened next?" enquired the bishop.

"Perhaps Alice felt she did not deserve Philip's love, perhaps she was seized with remorse. All we know is that she let herself slip into the Thames, and drowned."

"May the Lord receive her in his arms," murmured the bishops. "And give him peace."

On Saturday evening Sir Robert, Lady Constance, Margery, Philip and Sir Nicholas were settled in the elegant, high-ceilinged rooms which had been provided for them in the Palace of Whitehall. A blazing fire burned in the large hearth; on the table were a brilliantly white tablecloth of Flanders linen, silver tableware, crystal goblets from faraway Venice, and from the King's kitchens dishes so fine that even the curmudgeonly Margery had to approve: green lentil soup, purée of white Normandy onions, faggots of boar meat flavoured with mint, spiced game pie, piglet stuffed with chestnuts and ginger, yellow and red blancmanges, plums stewed in rose-water with cream. And all this accompanied by fragrant Rhenish wine, as clear as crystal.

The dinner was jovial and, as happens among old friends, an unceasing recollection of events which had bound them together over the years. But when the servants had cleared the table, and left only wine and marzipan sweetmeats, Lady Constance turned to Sir Nicholas: "Now tell me about Queen Kathryn."

"What do you want to know?"

"Everything, from the beginning. The true story."

Margery rose, placed upright a glass which had overturned on the table cloth, and went to bolt the door. "For caution's sake," she declared. "Here even the walls have ears."

Eventually she sat down on a bench in front of the fire. She muttered to herself: "Already my bones are aching, from head to foot. The London air."

"Deadly," joked Sir Robert – but he said it with affection, perhaps because the woman reminded him of the mother he no longer had. Margery shook her head, the lips curved in a smile: she in her turn was fond of Sir Robert.

And while Lady Constance wrapped a cloth around a hot brick to put under her feet, he handed her a goblet of spiced wine: "Warm yourself with this," and seated himself next to her. The others arranged themselves around, anxious to learn more.

Margery Ackworth

London, Palace of Whitehall

It was difficult to tell Margery Ackworth's age, a strong energetic woman, smelling of washing done with cinders. She had brightly coloured cheeks and a rubicund face, with fine red veins under her pale blue eyes. Only her gnarled hands, stray wisps of grey hair which escaped from under her bonnet, and slightly swollen heels, betrayed her age. It was she who had brought up the little Constance from the time that the latter had lost her mother, and had taught her how to behave and to write a few words before her father brought in a tutor.

When the young girl had gone to court, she had gone with her, as she had done when she had got married: from that day, with equal dedication, she had extended her good will to Sir Robert, even helping him when he ran into difficulties with his enquiries: with her maternal air, she managed to draw out from anyone their closest secrets, and then passed them on to him.

"Tell us all about Queen Kathryn, from the beginning," repeated Lady Constance.

"From when King Henry first came to know her?" enquired Sir Nicholas

"We know what everyone knows," replied Lady Constance. "That she had been brought to court by her uncle, Sir Thomas Howard, Duke of Norfolk, to be a maid-of-honour to the king's fourth wife, Anne of Cleves, but that the marriage was never consummated and was annulled after a few months. By the way, I have always wanted to know what happened to poor Anne."

Sir Nicholas laughed and helped himself to more wine: in such convivial moments the soldier that he had become gave way to the young friend of former times, the one who had protected Robert during their studies at Cambridge and who had been best man at their wedding. "First I shall recount the comedy. The tragedy afterwards."

He cleared his throat: "Well, two years after the death of his third wife, the much loved Jane Seymour, the king sent Hans Holbein to all the principalities on the Continent to paint noblewomen and propose marriage to them on his behalf. 'You would become Queen of England' the ambassadors promised these young ladies. But they, being fully aware of the fate which had befallen Henry's other wives, one after the other declined the offer."

Sir Robert interrupted: "It appears that the lovely Queen Cristina of Denmark replied to the English ambassador 'If I had two heads, I would gladly sacrifice one for the King of England.' "

Sir Nicholas nodded, sipping his wine: "Only one, Duchess Anne of Cleves, no longer very young, with little property to her name and sheltered from the world in an isolated province, showed herself ready. Perhaps because he was tired of travelling around Europe in search of eligible but reluctant young ladies, Holbein depicted her as younger than her years and her face unmarked by smallpox. But when Henry met her in person he flew into a rage: 'I could never love her, free me of this German mare,' he snarled, in front of the whole court. He ordered his chancellor Thomas Cromwell to find pretexts for escaping the commitment; for her part the timid and submissive Anne had the good sense not to object and this saved her life, and the king married the very young Kathryn with whom meanwhile he had fallen desperately in love."

"That's right. And she betrayed him," commented Lady Constance

"Almost immediately: but he noticed nothing. He called her his 'rose without thorns'. 'The purest of lilies, and you see how she loves me!' he would say, while the courtiers sniggered behind his back. He was happy, grew years younger. Now that the wound on his leg had apparently healed, he had started to ride again, to go hunting, and enjoy the smell of the forests and animals as he had thirty years before. And at night, Kathryn was a passionate lover."

"Kathryn Howard, wasn't she a cousin of Anne Boleyn?" observed Margery.

"Indeed. And when Kathryn was left an orphan," continued Sir Nicholas, "Sir Thomas Howard entrusted her to the care of his aunt, the aged dowager duchess Agnes Howard. There, in the delightful countryside of Horsham, the girl grew up in complete freedom, but without education. Instead she had numerous suitors and various sentimental attachments which were not entirely blameless. Indeed, one of the girls who lived with her, another of the duchess' wards, told how at night the guardian locked them in the dormitory, but that they opened the door with a second key and enjoyed the company of the young men of the household."

He took another sip of wine and proceeded: "Henry Manox, the music master, Francis Dereham, a house guest. They danced, drank, perhaps no more. Kathryn, though, drew aside with her lover, Thomas Culpepper, pulled the curtains round the bed, and what happened behind these left little to the imagination."

The rich food, the warmth of the fire, the easy conversation between friends: it was pleasant to be together. But when the bells of London's hundred churches rang the hour for the evening prayers of Compline, Sir Nicholas rose swiftly to his feet: "It is time for me to return to my rooms, I bid you good night."

The others prepared to go to the royal chapel, where they would pray: 'Lord, we thank you for having brought this day to its close. Now that the shadows lengthen and evening approaches, pardon us for the sins we have committed, help us to forgive those who have sinned against us, and grant us rest of body and mind."

As Sir Robert took from the table his Book of Hours – a small, richly illuminated volume, a present from his tutor – , Sir Nicholas paused by the door: "Robert: tomorrow, Sunday, everyone at court will be attending divine service. But," and he knit his brow, a shadow of unease on his face, "the sovereign has ordered me to bring you to him on Monday morning, immediately after Terce prayers."

"I shall be ready."

"You will find him changed, he is not the man he was. Do you remember nine years ago, when he asked you to attend his then queen, Anne Boleyn, when she gave birth? He loaded you with honours. Now you will see how he has become, how shall I say, suspicious, spiteful. Malevolent. He will wish to hear about your investigation."

"I shall make my report."

"Beware of how you conduct yourself. Be careful."

"What do you mean?"

There was no reply. Sir Nicholas had already left.

"It is just a difficult moment."

London, Whitehall

Sir Robert did not like being at court, he felt ill at ease amidst the haughty nobles: "I never had teachers to teach me dancing or swordsmanship," he sometimes said, not without a degree of envy, "just study, and more study. The only pastime that I could afford was to swim with my friends in the river Cam."

So on Monday morning, anxious and ready well before the appointed hour, he prepared himself for the meeting with the king: while his assistant Philip read him again the latest notes on Matthew Tiler's murder, he finished putting on an elegant blue waistcoat embroidered with silver thread, his chain of office well polished by Margery, and the smart blue velvet cloak padded with rabbit fur, all of which Lady Constance had taken out of the chest to air the evening before.

"There we are," he whispered, while his wife removed an invisible speck of dust from his shoulder, Margery regarded him approvingly, and Philip carefully replaced the papers in order on the shelf.

The young Philip had been under Sir Robert's tutelage for some years now: when he was twelve years of age, his mother, a widow, had apprenticed him to him so that he might become a doctor. When she too died in an epidemic, Sir Robert and Lady Constance gained permission for him to remain in their family, and in time he had become both assistant and secretary to his tutor.

Tall, handsome, the young man had thick chestnut hair, and dark eyes. The nose and lips were well shaped, with a certain melancholy in the lines of the mouth, a short and well-trimmed beard in a slender face. Margery kept him tidy, the shirts starched, the underclothes carefully darned.

He had always studied hard although his passions, more than medicine and crime, were poetry and music: often, at night, the old woman had found him by the hearth, composing ballads by the light of the braziers. Then she passed by him, and without saying anything, draped a shawl over his narrow shoulders. Tenderly: if her only child, a boy, had survived the plague, he would have been a little older than Philip. But she could not imagine him as an adult, her Benedict: those who die young don't grow old, she told herself, and in one's memory, they remain just as they were then…

Sir Nicholas led Sir Robert to the King's private chambers. The two of them climbed steep spiral stairs, made their way along cold corridors lit by torches on the walls and arrived in a hall where guards dressed in costumes of red and gold stripes, halberds crossed, stood in front of a nail-studded door made of dark oak, highly ornate towards the top. Sir Nicholas had himself announced, paid his respects to the sovereign and returned to the antechamber to wait for his friend.

A stale odour of enclosure and suffering permeated the King's private chamber. It was uncomfortably warm, the walls hung with heavy Bruges tapestries, worked in gold thread on red and blue backgrounds, and elaborately carved oak panels. Beside the king's bed, Joseph Godfrey, his personal physician, was finishing bandaging the huge, trunk-like legs; seated at a table, carefully rewinding the linen bandages, sat Joseph's daughter, Sarah, the young widow of the murdered merchant. Sir Robert recognized her, but she did not raise her eyes to look at him. 'And yet, she cannot have forgotten me,' he thought.

The King, stretched out on an imposing bed, was supported by numerous cushions and wore a thick bed-jacket embroidered in gold. 'He has become huge, the double of when I last saw him six years ago,' thought Sir Robert. In his own mind, he made a diagnosis: 'Watery eyes, flabby flesh. Swollen with poisonous humours, the blood is infected...'

"Sir Robert, my friend, you see what I have come to!" grumbled the king, with the surly gloominess of old age.

Sir Robert shook himself out of his private thoughts: "Sire," he murmured with a bow, "it is just a difficult moment. The whole of England regards you as the most powerful prince in Christendom."

The flattery had its desired effect. "What you say is true. Come and sit by me here. Everyone else, out!"

Sir Robert took a stool and sat down next to the bed. From close by the smell of the ailing body was nauseating, nor did the scents of the various ointments manage to conceal it.

"I don't like that Sarah," commented the King as Godfrey's daughter left the room, "She reminds me of that Boleyn witch." He shuddered, as if a ghost had passed by. "The same dark hair, the Spanish complexion, the enigmatic expression. If Godfrey weren't useful to me, I would gladly send her to the stake."

'The dead are silent,' thought Sir Robert. 'But Anne Boleyn haunts him still. Perhaps she returns in his dreams.'

The king sighed. "Sir Robert..."

"Sire."

"I have charged you with the investigation. How is it proceeding?"

Sir Robert gave an extensive report of events, from the finding of the body with the abandoned dagger at its side up to the post-mortem examination and the bizarre affair of the rings; from the unofficial enquiries made among the people of the neighbourhood to the list of people at court that he had in mind to question as soon as possible.

"Have you come to any opinion on the matter yet?"

"From the way in which the crime was committed, I would say that we are dealing with a vendetta."

"The city seethes with traitors, papists and robbers"

"If it had been practised thieves, they would have kept hold of the stiletto used to kill him: the hilt is of engraved silver, the weapon of a gentleman."

"Did it belong to the victim?"

"The widow did not recognize it." In fact, reflected Sir Robert in that moment, when I showed it to her, the woman, Sarah, was startled, hesitated – a shadow, a vision, seemed to pass over her eyes – , and only after that did she disclaim it.

Just then, accompanied by one of the King's gentlemen of the bedchamber, the servant attached to the cellars entered with some wine. The King tried some from a crystal goblet. "It's sour," he snarled, hurling it at the servant and hitting him in the face. The goblet fell to the floor and shattered;

the servant, an old man, begged pardon while picking up the pieces.

"Sir Robert, I wish you to bring your investigation to a speedy conclusion. Matthew, the dead man, was a good friend of mine."

"I shall do my best."

"I trust so. And do you know what an old hag prophesied about me as I was travelling back to Westminster? 'Henry,' she shouted, shaking a scrawny arm at me, 'Henry, in a little while you shall die and dogs shall lick up your blood'. I had her sent to the stake, the witch, and she didn't stop cursing me even as she was burning like a torch. Her cries still ring in my ears. And I am convinced that I too shall die soon."

Sir Robert shook his head, but refrained from saying 'It is something that happens to us all, sooner or later'.

"He should have died then..."

London, Whitehall

The king was now observing him through half-closed eyes, reduced to thin slits in the glutinous fat of the face. The room was fiery-hot, the closeness to the irascible sovereign uncomfortable. Sir Robert's cheeks were burning, his forehead bathed in sweat, his mind confused. The king's voice seemed to reach him from far away.

"Do you wish to know why I have decided that you lead the investigation? Why I have appointed you as my special coroner?"

"Sire?" he managed to reply.

"Because I had a clear recollection of your inquest six years ago, when you came to London and discovered that a servant of my queen Anne Boleyn's had been killed by a common whore, who, what is more, was also blind. No-one would have suspected her, but you brought her to justice."

Sir Robert ought to have explained that the details of the affair were very different: that the young woman was of noble birth and had lost her sight as the result of a tragedy. That the servant, William Crooks, one of the king's spies, was a scoundrel who molested her, taking advantage of her blindness. That he, Sir Robert, convinced of her innocence, had not only failed to bring her to justice but had connived at her escape to France. But he was afraid and refrained from speaking.

The sovereign continued: "And I remember too the inquest regarding the landlord of an ale-house in Bury St Edmund's, which the Duke of Norfolk told me about at the time. In my opinion it was a stroke of genius on you part: it would please me to hear you recount the story."

Sir Robert swallowed, pulled out a cloth, wiped the sweat from his face: "It was an interesting case. The man was found at the foot of the steps leading down to his cellar, where the barrels were kept. Dead, head injured, clearly the result of a fall. When the magistrate took me to see the corpse, the lad there declared: 'He was dead drunk.' In fact he smelt of beer, but I noticed that his shirt, beard and hair were all soaked with beer."

"And that made you have doubts," prompted the king: leaning towards Sir Robert, to hear him tell the story, he was as happy as a child.

"Yes, and on performing the *post-mortem* examination, I found that he had drowned, in beer. From which I deduced that the skull had been broken later."

"At which point you had to start making enquiries."

"So I began asking around: a brewer who supplied the landlord with beer revealed to me that for some time the man had complained to him that the barrels he received were not as full as before. 'That's not possible,' the brewer had replied. 'Keep an eye on your cellar, have it watched: you'll see that it is not I who am robbing you.' But even keeping watch day and night had proved fruitless, and the level of beer continued to go down. Eventually the landlord discovered his assistant somewhat tipsy, coming out of the hut which stood against the wall of the ale-house. They were heard to argue, the day after the landlord was found dead."

"And so you..."

"I realized that the solution to the mystery must be connected in some way to the hut. I went there accompanied by guards. We found a small bed, neat and tidy, a brazier with an iron lid, a chamber pot under the bed and a jug of beer on the shelf. All perfectly in order."

"No proof, then. Yet you..."

"But tapping on the wall of the wall of the hut which flanked the ale-house, we noticed that the sound was different at the base. We discovered there a brick which could be removed."

"And behind the brick..."

"...there was a pipe, with which the lad had helped himself directly from the cellar."

"And when the old landlord uncovered the trick..."

"... the lad pushed him against a fermentation vat, held his head under, then feigned the fall. That was all."

"Ah!" sighed the King, falling back again on his cushions. "I envy you, you know. Your work is much pleasanter than mine. For my part, all that I am able to do nowadays is put down rebellions and send people to the scaffold. In the long run that becomes, how should we put it, tedious."

What to say? Sir Robert searched for the right words: "Get better, my lord, return to governing, to administering justice in our cities. Do you remember how the people applauded as you passed by? They loved you. Those good days will return, Sire."

The sovereign shook his head. "Pour me some wine, have some yourself too."

The wine was exquisite. Sir Robert pondered the cause of the earlier outburst. The reason for the unexpected attack on poor Sarah. The ferocity with which the King had condemned his best friends to the block. Was he suffering from the French disease? That would have explained the sores on the legs. There was a glint of madness in the eyes: was he losing his mind?

Sipping his wine, the King continued. "No, my friend, there will be no more good days." He talked now as in a daydream. "I remember marrying my fifth wife, Kathryn, in the manor in Oatlands, in Surrey. That day she looked beautiful in her dress of white brocade, her hair silky, the colour of copper, falling down over her shoulders as befits virgins, her skin clear, her eyes a luminous blue, full of love as she looked at me, then cast down in modesty. And later, that night! She asked me to make love to her again and again. 'She's in love with me,' I thought. What had I done, I, almost an old man, to deserve such a gift of heaven. I worshipped her with all the devotion due to a virgin – Kathryn was my youth restored. O how I loved her!"

Now an unbelievable, pathetic sight unfolded: lying back on his cushions the sovereign started to cry. "A few weeks after the wedding I had to go back to London to greet the new Spanish ambassador and to convene the Privy Council. I was to have stayed away for several days; instead, I managed to get away sooner. I galloped into the castle courtyard, handed over my horse to the stableman and rushed to her. The dreadful Lady Rochford – wife of George Boleyn, that cursed family – , placed herself in front of the room.

'The Queen is sleeping, Sire'.

I was alarmed. 'Is she ill?'

'Oh no, she's just a little indisposed, but it is better that she stays in bed for a while'."

By then the King's eyes had become bloodshot. "Damnation! I should have died then... Do you want to know what her little indisposition was? Who was in bed with her having the time of his life?"

Sir Robert looked at him aghast.

"One of my gentlemen of the bedchamber," roared the King, "One with whom I had been hunting, who had shared my table. Do you understand? He who had been her lover during her time at Horsham: Thomas Culpepper!"

So it was Thomas Culpepper. Sir Robert had a moment of panic: sharing a ruler's secret is dangerous, certain confidences can mean death. A good pretext for sending him to the gallows if he didn't solve the case of the merchant. He seemed to feel the hangman's noose tightening around his neck.

As the King had stopped speaking, he raised his eyes to look at him. Henry seemed to be dozing off. Sir Robert tried to think: he had to do something quickly. On a shelf he saw some jars containing coloured powders, some of which were forbidden by the Church: wormwood, amanita, mandrake, hemlock, belladonna. And then pots of ointments and potions, some with the wax seal still unbroken: extract of nettle for bringing down temperature, aconite for earache, marshmallow for reducing catarrh, ash root powder for 'bowel movements', oil of scorpion for breaking down kidney stones. Amidst these a small crystal phial with the label '*Acetum – vinaigre*'. Yes, vinegar would do. He reached for it, poured out a little of the amber-coloured liquid in a small bowl, added some water, dipped in a cotton cloth, wrung it out, bent over the king, and gently wiped his face.

Henry jumped, opened his eyes, a startled expression on his face. "What the devil are you doing?"

Sir Robert smiled. "What you asked me to do before you drifted off."

"Meaning?"

"To freshen you a little. Then while I was preparing the vinegar and water and finishing the story of the brewer of Bury St Edmunds, you fell asleep."

"While you were speaking about the brewer... And I have been asleep since then?"

"Like an infant in the cradle, Sire, if you will forgive the expression."

The King's face relaxed. "I must have been dreaming. And did I talk in my sleep?"

"If you had done so, I should have heard."

In the garden of the Palace of Whitehall, right next to the King's room, there stood a tall tree. It was raining, a strong wind had arisen, and now the outer branches tapped like fingers against the small thick glass panes. The King shivered, Sir Robert removed his cloak and placed it over the outstretched legs. "I shall not forget this," mumbled Henry. He closed his eyes, and this time fell properly asleep.

As he left the room, feeling a little ashamed of having deceived his King, Sir Robert paused at the doorway, contemplate what remained of a once-great ruler. 'He was right,' he said to himself, 'he should have died then. Death would have been more dignified'.

"My mother called it common sense..."

London, Whitehall

When Sir Robert left the sovereign, he found Sir Nicholas waiting for him in the antechamber, worried. "You have been with him a long time. May I ask how it went?"

"We spoke."

"About the investigation?"

"Of that too. I told him everything I knew."

"How did he react?"

Sir Robert felt suddenly exhausted, sat down on a bench to catch his breath, his back against the wall: "Nicholas, not now, not here. However, the sovereign wished the enquiry to be concluded as speedily as possible."

"That means we must start the interrogations immediately."

"But not in the law chambers, I beg you. I hate those places with their cold draughts, filthy windows, the comings and goings of clerks in their black half-gloves."

"I had foreseen that. I have arranged for a study to be made available to you in the west wing of the palace, not far from your own rooms."

There they went. The study had a single window with shutters half-closed. In the shadows, a ray of sunlight revealed a table standing on a platform, covered with a thick woven cloth of bright blue and red. Behind the table a bench with arm-rests, and three high-backed chairs; in front were two low chairs and some stools. The fire was out, the walls cold. On the table some goose quills, some sheets of paper, a glass ink pot with a silver lid, a sand-glass, and on a stand a New Testament in red leather with a gold enamel cross on the cover.

Sir Nicholas threw open the blinds and called someone to light the fire. "The room is small, it will soon be warm."

Two servants arrived: one crouched by the fire to arrange dry straw and wood shavings that he drew out of a sack, the other lit this with his torch. Bright flames sprang up on which the two placed some logs of scented apple wood.

"Nicholas, if you could be present for the interviews, it would be a great help."

"I'll be here. And would you like your wife to here too?"

"She and Margery have a better sense of smell than a Norman bloodhound. They have their secret ways of inquiring, and often, when they show me a trace…"

"Sense of smell, you say? My mother used to call it 'common sense', what you men lack, she said."

So the two women were invited to join them. In order not to be to obtrusive, they would be seated in the darkest corner of the room, in the shadows, and they would pretend to be busy with their endless embroidery.

All over London snow continued to fall, and through the window a pale iridescent light entered the study. Sir Robert was seated between Sir Nicholas, who was reading a document, and Philip, who was arranging ink pot, quills and papers.

"We can begin," said Sir Robert.

Out of a case he took a pair of spectacles, round and mounted in bone, put them on, adjusted them with his forefinger, and smoothed with his hand the note that Sir Nicholas had given him beforehand: "The people of the court that we need to interview, that is those who did not stay in the Palace of Whitehall on the night of the crime, are as follows: the young Sir James, according to the captain of the guard. You recall? He had seen him leave in the afternoon, but not re-enter. Then the doctor Joseph Godfrey, his daughter Sarah, his sister Esther. Washerwomen, servants, kitchen boys, some cooks. The Duke of Norfolk, whom we certainly cannot interrogate, and his mistress, the beautiful Elizabeth Holland. The Duchess Agnes Howard, perhaps Lady Jane Rochford, lady-in-waiting to Kathryn."

He sighed. "And if we don't find the killer amongst these, there are a mere hundred thousand inhabitants of London to question."

"Sir Barnaby Lowell, the Gentleman of the Bedchamber to the king, can be excluded. He had already left the city to make his way to Scotland, in the forces of the Duke of Norfolk. The Scots have again crossed the border and taken Berwick Castle. They have burnt farms, seized livestock, raped women. I would not wish to be in their place when Norfolk arrives there."

"What about Sir James?"

"You met him when he accompanied us to Southwark, the morning after the murder, and he felt ill: he's a good lad, not one who goes abroad at night stabbing old men."

"Even good lads can kill, if it suits them."

"You can always summon him later."

Sir Robert agreed: he had liked the young man, with the helmet above an innocent face, almost childlike, and that sudden distress when confronted with death. Even if, he reflected, there may have been something personal in that reaction: "Margery has heard rumours of a friendship between the young man and the victim's young wife," he said.

"Gossip. He, a gentleman of the royal household, she a daughter of the king's physician, at some court feast they will have danced together, that's all."

"Probably so. But let's keep them in mind." He gestured to Philip, who was taking notes.

"Well, then. Let us now clear the field of the ordinary folk, then pass to the ladies and gentlemen of the court."

Sir Nicholas gave orders for the washerwomen to be called.

Accompanied by soldiers there entered three women wearing course linen bonnets, their sleeves still rolled up, white smocks over their plain woollen frocks, their faces bright and good-natured.

"Ladies," said Sir Robert, motioning them to sit down. Their eyes opened wide, they looked at each other, then burst into laughter. Exclaimed the oldest of the three: "Beg pardon! No-one has ever called us 'ladies' before!"

They sat down. Sir Robert and Sir Nicholas took turns to ask them questions: "On the night between the seventeenth and eighteenth of January, the night when the merchant Matthew Tiler met his death, do you remember at what hour you left the Palace?"

"Soon after we had removed the tablecloths from the tables after the royal banquet. We put them in their baskets, so that the day after we could wash them."

"And where did you go?"

"Where do you think we went after washing clothes all day?"

"Did anyone see you return to your homes?"

"In Southwark? At night people there sleep."

"Your men can bear witness for you?"

"Them? We are sailors' wives, sir. Who knows where they were, or who they were sleeping with, in that moment!"

When the women were led out Sir Robert looked despondently at Sir Nicholas, who stretched wide his arms in response. Lady Constance emerged from the shadowy corner: "In the space of a few hours Margery will know all about them and their husbands," she reassured them.

"And about their respective families," confirmed Margery. "I'll tell you tomorrow."

She would not disappoint.

A dead end

London, Whitehall

Seven days had elapsed since the night of the crime and the investigation had still failed to make progress. Sir Robert had sought to speak to the people of Southwark, but no-one had seen anything, no-one knew anything, and even if they had known something, they would not have told him, 'an outsider, perhaps one of Norfolk's spies', as they had shouted him in the past, showing him their fists.

Even the interrogation of cooks, kitchen boys and servants from Whitehall had proved fruitless, and he felt enveloped in a fog denser than that which covered London in that January of snow and discontent. Unfriendly people in an unfriendly city, the time granted him by the sovereign gradually shrinking, and a sense of powerlessness and ungovernable fear dominating his thoughts.

When that evening he, Lady Constance, Sir Nicholas, Philip and Margery met together after dinner, his hope was that at least the others had discovered something. Lady Constance recognized his frustration – they did not need words between them –, and while the company huddled round the fire, she cast a supplicating eye at Margery.

"Sir Robert," Margery then said, "perhaps I have some news for you. This morning I happened to meet someone in the flower market, the one near the Tower – I was looking for a packet of seeds for the garden in Cambridge."

"We all know your fondness for markets, Mistress Ackworth," commented Sir Nicholas. He sipped some wine and and stretched his legs in front of the hearth: he foresaw that the story would be a long one.

"It was not a large market, this one. But I was fortunate, there I met one of the cooks from Whitehall Palace – you would not believe the number of people who work in that kitchen, and the waste."

"But with all the leftovers from the king's table, the servants keep many a poor family from starving," added Sir Nicholas.

"That is true."

Briefly reduced to silence, Margery then continued: "Well, this woman strongly resembled a friend of mine from Sunbury, the very picture of her, but younger, without wrinkles. My friend was a cook too, she was at Baynard's Castle. I passed by there yesterday, it's that building in pink marble with battlements, by the river."

"The London residence of the Yorks, one of the loveliest houses in the city," commented Sir Nicholas.

"Yes. My friend was called Joan, Joan Taylor, daughter of a tailor. She had come to London when she married a farrier from here, a certain Martin Allen, who lived in the district of Westcheap."

'If only Margery would come to the point,' thought lady Constance. 'But if we try to hurry her, she curls up like a hedgehog and won't say another word.'

"So I stared at her," continued Margery. "She asked me why, and I told her that she looked just like my friend Joan Taylor from Sunbury. All was clear: 'Sunbury in Surrey? But then that's Joan, my grandmother!' she cried. She hugged me, told me about herself, about life at court, there's a lot I could tell you about that. The woman is called Cecily, daughter of Margaret Gavell and granddaughter of Joan Taylor. She's married to Thomas Claybrook, the king's blacksmith..."

"And you brought the conversation round to our investigation and discovered something very, very interesting," prompted Lady Constance gently.

"I believe so. She knew Matthew Tiler the merchant because she lives near him, south of London Bridge. 'No-one can explain the crime, everyone in the neighbourhood is talking about it,' she said. Do you want to know what I think?"

"Yes, of course," I replied.

"I think that the killer mistook him for someone else. He was frightened by what he'd done and ran away. And he's in hiding who knows where."

Margery paused to catch her breath, giving Sir Robert chance to ask: "She spoke to you about the family?"

"She told me that four of them lived together in that house: the dead man – and here Margery made the sign of the cross–, and Joseph Godfrey, a kind of doctor who uses herbal remedies. His daughter Sarah, a nice girl who helps him, several times she's treated her, Cecily. Then there was the doctor's sister, Esther, and it seems that she is rather a nasty piece of work. She hated that poor Tiler, and she hates Sarah."

"Did she say why?"

"She referred to a marriage: she said that her brother had promised her to the merchant, but then he had changed his mind and offered him his daughter instead. There's something to do with a will, and a question of blackmail, perhaps involving Queen Kathryn, if I have understood correctly. But by the time I was getting to the main point, we had arrived at Whitehall and I couldn't ask any more questions. We'll be seeing each other again soon though, she has pressed me on this, and now that I know her I can go and see her in the kitchens and also speak with the other women."

Margery looked at Lady Constance as if to ask 'did I do well?'.

Constance nodded, and Sir Robert said: "Well done, Margery, that's a good lead! Very very interesting. Nicholas, is there time to summon Godfrey, sister Esther and his daughter Sarah for tomorrow morning? I have already requested from the church courts all relevant documents on the Godfrey and Tiler families, I trust that they will be with me soon."

He concluded: "As you can see, if Esther Godfrey hated the merchant, may be the murderer has always been in that house."

Sir Nicholas went to the door, called a guard, gave him an order and returned to sit with his friends.

Blackmail

London, Whitehall

Attention moved to Lady Constance, who seemed anxious to add something to her governess' words: "As for me," she said, "at lunch I found myself seated next to Joseph Godfrey himself. I can't say I liked him. He's burly, thick-lipped, with a double chin, and he speaks with such a resounding voice that the very rafters ring. Arrogant. With a show of false modesty he confided to me that he was the king's favourite physician, and the best in all London, but added that if the sovereign's condition should grow worse, as a foreigner he might be condemned to the scaffold. 'But I am religious, a man of faith,' he thundered. 'All the better,' I let slip, 'so when they hang you, you will go happily to heaven'."

"So he said nothing further to you," supposed Sir Robert.

"He did not take offence. 'I was jesting,' I told him, and gave him a tap on the arm. 'Everyone knows how clever you are.' It worked."

While Sir Robert was looking puzzled at her, she added: "He even paid court to me a little. He declared: 'If I had known you before, I would have honoured you with a proposal of marriage.' 'We all have occasion to regret things,' I replied to him.

At this point he became a fount of information: on himself, on his daughter. Listen to this: on the evening of the murder Sarah was not at court."

"And why not, if she always goes there with her father? About her we knew little, that she married the old man, and that she was a friend of Queen Kathryn: but now here is something interesting. Ah, women!" exclaimed Sir Robert.

He turned to his friend: "Nicholas, this morning I did not have time to tell you that the sovereign had spoken to me of his wife Kathryn."

"Tell me now."

What caused Sir Robert to hesitate, perhaps a sudden gleam in Sir Nicholas' eyes? "Well, he just mentioned it," he replied vaguely. "I would rather that you told me. You see, I discovered that Jane Boleyn, Lady Rochford, one of the ladies-in-waiting to Queen Kathryn, is a prisoner in the Tower, so I shall not be able to question her. But without disturbing the waters too much, can one know the reason? Besides: how did a merchant's wife come to be so intimate with the queen? And once at dinner, when we were waiting for Constance to arrive from Cambridge, you told me that Kathryn herself is confined to Syon Abbey, accused of high treason."

He raked his fingers to his hair: "I beg you, continue from where you stopped the other night, tell me about her and Thomas Culpepper – about the blackmail, if there ever was such, that the cook, Cecily, referred to. After all, if I am to move in court circles, I must also know how matters stand."

Sir Nicholas appeared to hesitate. He rose, went to the window. Another storm, the sky suddenly dark, and drops of rain which ran down the small bright stained-glass panes. He turned and seated himself again. "It is not a question of gossip here, as with was with the poor Anne of Cleves: all our necks are at risk if anything should go beyond this room. But as it is so important for you, under pledge of secrecy, I can tell you."

He requested from Margery the cross that she wore round her neck, on which each of them in turn took an oath, and he began to speak: "At court everyone knew about the queen's affair. The king heaped on her gifts, jewels, precious stones. He would say: 'I wish to reward her for her purity, for her innocent love.' But the Chancellor Thomas Audley confided to me that Kathryn had come to him one morning with a pearl casket in her hands, her hair loose about her shoulders. Beautiful, so young, she was like a child on a Christmas morning. Opening the lid to reveal a number of jewels she had asked him: 'Can I have some money in exchange for these without the king knowing?'

So Audley had asked her why she needed the money. 'It's that I have to give it to someone', and bursting into tears she showed him a letter."

"From a poor relative?" asked Sir Robert.

"Joan Bulmer, an old companion from the time when they were both at Horsham under the tutelage of the old Howard duchess. The letter was undated, written in a clumsy hand on a cheap piece of paper. I recall its content perfectly. It said:

'Lady Kathryn, you will surely remember me, as we lived together at Horsham and Lambeth palace under the Duchess of Norfolk and shared the same bedroom. We had friends in common: Henry Manox, Francis Dereham and the handsome Thomas Culpepper, whom you will certainly not have forgotten. My current life in the North is hard. I would that you call me to your service in London. I beseech you, I know how kind and generous you are. If you refuse, I don't know what may happen.'

"But if you refuse: what wickedness in those words," commented Lady Constance. "And what happened next?"

Before Sir Nicholas could reply, one of Norfolk's men arrived to summon him on some important matter concerning the king. Sir Robert reminded Sir Nicholas: "We meet in my study tomorrow morning, when we shall interrogate the three Godfreys. And I shall have in my hands, I hope, all the documents relating to the two families."

"Including Tiler's will, if there is one."

"All three Godfreys should prove interesting, but particularly the young widow: don't you find that there is something disquieting about that woman?"

The astrologist doctor

London, Whitehall, Sir Robert Kytchyn's study

The medical astrologist Joseph Godfrey was exactly as Lady Constance had described him: large, conceited, arrogant. It was nearly the Sixth Hour when he arrived, late, filling the room with his massive frame. The dark eyes under the frowning brow looked around suspiciously. The nostrils were flared as if to scent danger, and the ears ready to catch whispers and rumours.

Before Sir Robert had invited him to do so he sat down in front, rested an elbow on the table, bellowed: "As you can see I am here, even though I don't understand why you have summoned me."

"I thank you for coming," Sir Robert replied gently.

"Very well. But I must warn you: my time is precious, the king awaits me."

"We are all grateful for all the care that you lavish on our sovereign."

Godfrey had not expected such graciousness. Brought to a halt, he stroked his beard. He asked: "So, what can I do for you?"

"Talk to us about Matthew Tiler the merchant. Tell us about him."

The man grew wary: "Tell you what?"

"What you want. I leave it to you to decide. I did not know him. For example, do you think he and I could have been friends?"

"How can I say… He was older than you."

"While his wife, your daughter, is very young."

Godfrey was silent, a flash of suspicion in his eyes grown suddenly sullen. What was he insinuating, where was he trying to lead him with those questions?

"You must have had a good relationship with Matthew," continued Sir Robert.

"Excellent. He was shrewd in his business and friend of the king's."

"How did he come to know your daughter?"

'What has all this to do with me?' wondered Godfrey. And why was that pale youth, a secretary perhaps, writing down everything he said?'

"I don't recall," he grumbled.

"Was it the merchant who presented you to the king?"

"The king was pleased about it."

"We do not doubt it."

Sir Robert said nothing, observed Godfrey for a few moments and, when he proceeded, his tone had become slightly less amiable: "Do you recall where you were on the night between the seventeenth and eighteenth of January?"

"The night in which Matthew was killed? I stayed at court, the sovereign wanted me with him. I think you know that I am the only one who can give him any relief from his pain."

"How did your learn of the murder?"

"A baker's apprentice came to the gate of Whitehall, he alerted the guards."

"Your daughter was there too?"

"I wouldn't know. Perhaps. Or, if there was a moon, she might have been in the meadows with the dogs, collecting herbs."

Sir Robert briefly drummed his fingers on the table: "When conducting the *post mortem* I noticed that Tiler's hands had been badly burnt. Do you know how it happened?"

"There was a fire, some time ago."

"How long ago?"

The man hesitated: "I'm not exactly sure. A little while after we had gone to live with him. I remember that the room where he was sleeping went up in flames, but that he escaped with his life. I treated his body with ointments of my own creation, but I could only ease the pain in his hands, which had burnt down to the bone."

Sir Robert persisted stubbornly: "How did the fire start?"

"There was a trace of oil on the floor, an upset lantern by the bed. It was early morning, Matthew was still asleep, the blankets were the first to catch fire."

"The rest of the room?"

"The flames attacked the chests of drawers and the shutters, Matthew managed to throw sand on them from the bucket that we keep in every room – in Southwark fires are common."

"And when you returned home?"

"I found him unconscious on the landing. Afterwards I found that he had snuffed out the candle as every night, but that the lantern was from the kitchen and should not have been in his room."

"Who had taken it there?"

"He didn't say."

"Did he suspect someone?"

"I didn't ask him."

"Where were you?"

"Out with a patient."

"And your daughter?"

"Usually at that time she's with Matthew, but that morning she had left early, soon after me. My sister Esther had asked her to go and buy some fish at Billingsgate."

"And she, your sister?"

"She was... she said she was outside talking to a neighbour."

"You asked her because you suspected her?"

Godfrey looked down.

"You were guests in the merchant's house?"

"He had wanted to continue living there even though he was not without money. Soon my sister and I shall move to a house more fitting to my present station, on a street which crosses Paternoster Row."

Sir Robert's voice became harder: "Paid for by Tiler?"

"Yes. But..."

"Yes or no?"

"What are you insinuating?"

"Yes or no?"

"Yes."

A note of jealousy

London, Whitehall, Sir Robert Kytchyn's study

Perhaps there came into Sir Robert's mind the words that Godfrey had addressed to Constance: 'If I had made your acquaintance sooner, I should have honoured you with a proposal of marriage.' Perhaps he was stirred by a pang of jealousy. The fact is that he whispered in Sir Nicholas' ear: "Now comes the best part."

Sir Nicholas smiled and shook his head, looking fixedly at Godfrey as his friend proceeded. "Do you know whether Tiler had named you in his will?"

The man turned purple.

Sir Robert drew a paper from a leather folder: "I have received this from the Ecclesiastical Court, where it was deposited. Allow my secretary to read it to you:

In the name of God, Amen. The fifth day of January 1541, in the thirty-third year of Henry, King of England.

I, Mathew Tiler, citizen and merchant of the City of London, being sound of mind and memory, declare and record here in writing my will regarding my worldly goods:

First, I commend my soul to God Almighty, my Creator and Redeemer, to the Blessed Virgin Mary, and to all the saints, and request that my body be buried in the churchyard of St Mary Overy, to which parish I belong... etc.

I leave ten pounds sterling to the rector of the said church so that masses may be offered for my soul... etc. I leave to each of the four orders of mendicants of the City of London... to those held in the prisons of London... to the sick paupers... to thirty poor girls of good reputation, for their marriage.. .to the destitute of the City of London...

I leave to the parish of St Gregory's, so that masses may be celebrated in memory of my first wife, Margaret...

I leave to the Guild of Merchants my goods as follows...

I leave to my wife Sarah, whom I wish to reward for her affection towards me, all the pearls that I possess, both large and small, and all my personal effects listed below...

To my father-in-law the sum of 50 gold sovereigns and the same to his sister Esther.

The executors of my will are... etc.

In witness to all the above, I put my seal to these provisions, recorded in London on the day and in the year cited above.'

Faithfully, Matthew Tiler, Merchant on London

Sir Nicholas took the papers from Philip's hands and waved it in front of the doctor: "Doctor Godfrey, were you aware of the existence of this will?"
The man looked around, as if searching for a way of escape.

Sir Robert pressed him further: "We have heard Matthew Tiler described as a kind-hearted man, which is evident from what we have just read. So who could bear him a grudge?"

There was no reply. Godfrey frowned and Sir Robert had the impression that he was struggling to remember something. He repeated the question: "Who might hate your son-in-law? Perhaps someone close to him?"

Godfrey looked at him fearfully.

"Perhaps someone in the family?"

Godfrey's face had turned violet. He clenched his fists as if he intended to hit someone. His seat clattered to the floor as he leapt to his feet: "I have to go," he mumbled, and rushed out of the room.

"Because she's dead."

London, Whitehall, Sir Robert Kytchyn's study

Sir Nicholas turned to Sir Robert: "What do you make of that?"

"A fire in the early morning, and everyone out of the house at that uncommon hour. Him left alone. An overturned lantern, not his, and perhaps someone who bore him a grudge. As I thought, it is the dead man who will lead us to his killer."

With a brushing of skirts on the floor Lady Constance and Margery emerged from the shadows and approached the table.

Sir Robert asked: "Well ladies, what are your thoughts on that?"

"He was unsettled by your questions, he was afraid of something from the very start," replied Lady Constance. "And knowing how the sister hated Tiler and his young wife, that fire sounds suspicious."

"Anyway we shall question this Esther closely: she must be here by now, in the ante-chamber, waiting to be summoned."

"It's rather late, would it not be wise to eat something?" suggested Margery.

There was good sense in this proposal, they could continue in the afternoon. Everyone stood up, Sir Nicholas stretched, Sir Robert glanced at how much Philip had written: "Very good," he said approvingly.

They left the study in order to announce the change of programme. But there was no-one waiting outside.

As they came back in the early afternoon, they were met by a slow-witted servant who had arrived breathless from the merchant's house:

"The sister of the doctor it seems that she can't come."

"How is that?" asked Sir Nicholas.

The servant scratched his head, apparently unable to make sense of the question.

"Why can't Doctor Godfrey's sister come?"

"Why... Because she's dead."

"How, where, when?" the others exclaimed.

"I know nothing," muttered the servant. He spread wide his arms and limped off.

So Sir Robert, Sir Nicholas and Philip went down into the courtyard, had their horses saddled and rode as briskly as the laboured breathing of Asklepius would allow to the late Matthew Tiler's dwelling.

When they arrived at London Bridge they dismounted and, holding the animals by the halter, crossed on foot in case the hustle and bustle around them unsettled the horses.

Indeed from the workshops on the wide-arched bridge came apprentices laden with sacks and boxes of different merchandise, some women exchanged news shouting across to one another from the windows of houses above the shops, carts pulled by oxen carried fruit, vegetables, game from the countryside to the city markets, and barrows loaded with fish and donkeys with baskets on their sides passed through the crowd alongside litter-bearers transporting elegant ladies.

Only after the bells of St Mary-le-Bow had sounded the curfew would the bridge grow quiet, and the streets deserted.

At the merchant's house more would be revealed.

In the merchant's house

London, Southwark

The merchant's house, where resided his wife, Sarah, the doctor Godfrey and his sister, did not differ from the other ramshackle dwellings in the borough except for the recently re-done thatched roof, the well-maintained white plaster, the door re-varnished in blue, the doorstep of new stone.
Outside stood some women with toddlers clinging to their skirts. The servant whom they already knew took their horses by the bridle and led them into the stalls behind the house.
"Take care with this one, or he'll kick you," warned Sir Robert, surrendering his mount, and it seemed as if the honest Asklepios reproved him with a look: "I said that so that he won't treat you roughly," he whispered in the horse's ear.
A kitchen maid showed them into a small room. Here everything bore witness to the old merchant's prosperity: a roaring blaze in the fire-place and the smell of good wood which permeated the room, a chest with cushions covered in blue and yellow satin, a seat with arm-rests, a silver candle-stick holding a lit candle of scented beeswax, heavy velvet curtains at the window to shield against draughts,

fine crockery and some pewter plates on the dresser behind the large oak table. This latter was covered with a Turkish rug in red and blue, and on a shelf stood prominently a German clock in gilded brass with signs of the Zodiac in blue: this could be heard ticking and after a while striking the hour.

Godfrey was seated at the table, in shirt and waistcoat, his head in his hands: the candlelight showed him absorbed in reading some papers. The face was pale, the eyes weary-looking, but the expression did not seem anxious. When he saw them come in, there was a moment of apprehension: but he recovered, stood up and thanked them for coming. The tone was different from the arrogance of the morning. 'He is not upset. His eyes aren't red, so he has not been crying. Moreover, he seems to be showing me more respect. Is he afraid?' wondered Sir Robert.
"My sister..." sighed Godfrey.
"What happened?"
"She must have fallen: she was lying at the foot of the stairs, with her neck broken."
"Where is she now?"
"We carried her upstairs, into the bedroom that she shared with me."
He took the candle and, shielding the flame with his hand, started to climb the dark wooden stairway. Sir Robert, Sir Nicholas and Philip groped their way after him, feeling the steps with their feet. Sir Robert noticed that the man's hand was trembling.

The upper storey consisted of two rooms, that of the merchant's and that of Godfrey's, which they entered. There they found two chests, a large one reinforced with wrought iron, and a second, smaller one in plain wood; a stand hung with clothes, a large bed, some shelves and, beneath the window, a cot-bed on which was lying a woman clad in black: tall, shrivelled, hair a dull grey, the mouth set sourly even in the repose of death.

Godfrey made a gesture with his hand, as if to introduce her: "My sister Esther," he said.

'Here is the woman who would have liked to marry the merchant,' thought Sir Robert. 'She would have been confident in that prospect. Then the other one takes him away from her, and she, who now hates them both, is obliged to live her life under the same roof. She complains about it to her brother, but where else can she go?'

While Godfrey stayed standing in the doorway, Sir Robert motioned to Sir Nicholas and Philip that they should look around. At the same time he himself knelt down next to the little bed, pressed his fingers against a vein in the woman's neck, lifted an eyelid, laid his ear against her chest. He took her head between his hands and carefully moved it from side to side; he pushed aside the clothing on the shoulders and examined her neck. He turned to Godfrey: "She's been dead for some hours. She fell down the stairs and broke her neck."

When he had heard this opinion, Godfrey seemed to relax. "You are knowledgeable in such matters."

"Quite so. Who found her?"

"I did, when I came back from your study."

"Who was in the house with her?"

"At that hour, nobody."

"Where was everyone?"

There was a flash of apprehension in Godfrey's eyes. Aware that Sir Robert would be able to verify what he said, the man replied: "I had sent the maidservant to the chemist's in

Cheapside to order some medicines, and sent my man to purchase something to drink."

"Where?"

"At the brewer's behind Tower Hill."

"And your daughter?"

"She had gone to attend a sick woman."

'He hasn't wept. He doesn't seem upset, and he was alone in the house with his sister,' Sir Robert told himself. 'In addition he stinks, there's an odour of fear about him.

He came up to him and took hold of his wrist: "You have some scratches here."

Godfrey made as if to hide his hand: "I hurt myself a few days ago."

"These scratches are recent." He approached the little bed again. "I should search all the room, but I shall limit myself to this."

He slid a hand under the pillow and pulled out some sheets of paper. Godfrey reached out to snatch them. Sir Robert took a step backwards, folded them up and calmly slipped them into Philip's bag. "Do you know anything about these papers?"

"Nothing." The man was clearly lying.

"They will be submitted as evidence to the Royal Court of Justice. You see, while I was moving her head, I heard the rustle of paper, so I realized that your sister was keeping something hidden beneath the pillow. Not in the chest, notice, where anybody could have searched for it, but under her own pillow. Then I saw the bruises on her neck, the sign that someone had held her by the throat. Godfrey, your sister's death was not an accident: someone pushed her down the stairs."

He looked him straight in the eye for some time: Godfey lowered his gaze.

Once they were outside, Philip asked "Do you think he could be the murderer?"

"Of the merchant and his own sister?"

"It would be quite a stroke for us..."

"And he would inherit the house and all the rest. It's another possibility, certainly."

He thought for some moments: "Listen, I know what I'll do: I'll make enquiries with the Guild of Physicians and Apothecaries to find out more about him."

Esther Godfrey

London, Whitehall

"So we have another death on our hands," grumbled Margery, as she and Lady Constance re-entered Whitehall through the gardens, after having attended a service in the church of St Margaret's close by Westminster Abbey. They walked briskly, enveloped in their fur-lined cloaks, the hoods well down to shelter their faces, the snow crunching under their boots.

"Sir Robert will give us the details when he returns from Godfrey's house. Do you have any news from your friend Cecily?"

"I would have liked to report her words yesterday evening, seeing that Sir Robert was to interview those two women this morning. But there was no time."

"What had she told you?"

"Esther Godfrey was advanced in years, never married, and her brother, Doctor Godfrey, had promised her to Matthew Tiler, the merchant, a rich widower. The lady had comforted herself with this prospect. Subsequently, though, Godfrey realized that the old man could introduce him into court. And there he would do well for himself, he was very capable, so everyone said."

"If he was so clever, why couldn't he arrange his own introduction?"

"Just think, he's not English. A foreigner, coming from Spain. Jewish, apparently. So what could he do? Give his daughter in marriage and gain the king's favour."

"And the sister?"

"You can imagine the tears, the scenes. But that is not all."

"Holy Mother of God, there's still more?"

"Cecily has told me that the three Godfreys were living in cramped rooms above a spice merchant's in the district of St Mary le Bow. So, after the marriage to Sarah, Matthew Tiler invited Joseph and Esther to go and live with him in his house in Southwark."

"And Esther hated Sarah and the poor Tiler. What did Godfrey know of this? And why ever, I wonder, this morning, did he flee, his face white with terror, when Sir Robert mentioned a will?"

The two women nodded at each other with an understanding gesture, like two hounds which had scented a new trail.

Their conversation was interrupted by the arrival from Southwark of Sir Robert, Sir Nicholas and Philip, who briefly recounted what they had discovered at the merchant's house.

Meanwhile a wind had arisen which threw up swirling clouds of snow, and Philip was paler than usual, his teeth chattering with the cold. Margery took him by the arm: "You are too lightly dressed. Come with me, I shall ask them to prepare you a good mulled wine with sage and cloves," she said, and led him towards the kitchen.

The Whitehall kitchens were huge, and crowded with people at work as the hour of dinner approached. Young kitchen boys, half naked in front of the hearths, stirred soups in large cauldrons suspended over fires in the enormous fireplaces, others turned spits on which sucking pigs were skewered, others plucked capons, hens, geese and ducks amidst showers of feathers. A towering fisherman deftly cleaned seafood of all kinds, while different cooks with large white aprons prepared sauces from a range of aromatic herbs – sandalwood, saffron – , or mulberry, and desserts with fruit and honey cakes. On the shelves a host of mortars, pestles, jars, tureens and jugs, and on hooks a variety of copper pans hanging in order of size.

Margery and Philip were greeted by a swell of voices and colours, delicate aromas and pungent odours.

"Forgive me for using you as a pretext for coming here, but I had to hear from my friend Cecily how much she knows about this new death," apologized Margery.

"I had thought as much," he replied with a smile.

Cecily – rosy faced, plump, bright eyes and an animated voice – , was intent on scolding a kitchen maid, but when the woman started to cry she muttered: "Come on, take heart, try to do better next time."

Then she saw Margery and came to meet her: "She's so careless, she makes a mess of everything. But she's expecting a baby and her husband was lost at sea. I would not send her away even if she set fire to the kitchen. But let's hope that she doesn't do that!"

She wiped her hands in her apron: "Dear Margery."

"Cecily, Master Philip is my master's assistant, he's perishing from the cold."

She had barely finished speaking before the woman led him into a smaller kitchen, sat him next to the fire and offered him a steaming beaker of wine.

"Smooth," commented Philip. "What is it?"

"Hippocras. We serve it to the king: red wine, honey, cinnamon. Drink it while it's hot."

There was some too for Margery, who seated herself with a sigh — after the walk from St Margaret's her legs were aching. She then looked around and asked with apparent indifference: "Have you heard about Godfrey's sister?"

Cecily crossed herself several times: "When she was alive she was really wicked, ready to make mischief for anyone, envious of that poor Sarah. She once said plain and clear that she would like to see her disgraced. But the brother too is not much better: in his own way, he loved his first wife and when she died he saw it as an act of spite on the part of the Good Lord, he became arrogant: if you have no money, he will not treat you."

Looking about her, Margery noticed the merchant's young widow seated on a bench at a corner table, opposite a servant, dressing her badly burned hand. The two girls were gossiping about something, under their breath, and laughing. This surprised Margery given Sarah's recent loss. The old woman thought that she would willingly surrender the last of her healthy teeth to know what they were discussing. Especially since she seemed to hear the words 'queen' and 'Kathryn'.

"So young, and so beautiful."

London, Whitehall

That morning a thick fog enshrouded the City of London, and the unwholesome stench of the mud and filth which bestrewed the streets reached even into the Palace of Whitehall.

"I keep thinking of the coming springtime, of how it will be in Cambridge," sighed Lady Constance, giving a final stitch to the shirt that she was darning. "I see those high skies, the birds circling in the evening..."

Sir Robert raised his eyes from his papers – he was pale, anxious: "I too need some home air. Would that I had never taken this accursed case!"

"You could not have done otherwise," said Philip. And tapping with his forefinger the papers that he was putting in order: "Here is proof of the hard work you have already completed. Now there only remains to be interviewed the merchant's wife, that Sarah Godfrey."

"I am expecting much from her. But we must hear her father again – that seems a most promising trail – , and other people in Southwark and at court. And in this next round I have decided to follow what I term my Method Number Two."

"Meaning?" asked Lady Constance.

"I will give the impression of following a particular path, and will make appear that I am going wrong. Everyone will rush to correct me, to give details, to incriminate others, to speak too much about themselves. How often have I seen someone guilty fall into the trap, say more than they intended, and in the end condemn themselves. I only hope that it can be accomplished swiftly."

He added: "Time and the king, there are my enemies. And shadows and obstacles at every step."

He did not know then how far the passage of days would prove him right.

And as if in answer, Sir Nicholas appeared at the door.

"Good morning to you all!"

He went to stand in front of the fireplace, his cloak and boots were soaked: "Cold and damp, outside. And I have heard that in few days' time I must head north with other soldiers to join Norfolk. The news from up there is bad."

He turned to Sir Robert: "So for your investigation you will have to report directly to King Henry."

"No!"

"Yes, indeed. And why are you so afraid? He is confident that you will solve the mystery before too long."

"And that's the point. He is confident, but also distrustful, vindictive. And the hatred of a king, remember... And if after all this time I haven't managed to find the truth, I ask myself: where have I gone wrong?"

With his habitual gesture he raked his fingers through his hair: "And then, Nicholas, if it is I who am obliged to report to the sovereign, if I have to reason with him, to think quickly, have to choose between truth, conjectures, lies... I who have none of the courtier's skills will need much more information from you. That at least you owe me."

Sir Nicholas removed his cloak and hung it on a hook to drip.

"Information? I'm ready to provide it."

Sir Robert went to sit at his friend's side, next to the fire: "Nicholas, how did the friendship between Sarah Godfrey and Queen Kathryn begin? Did she play the go-between with her lovers? And why has Lady Jane Rochford been shut in the Tower?"

He clasped his hands together as if imploring him to speak the truth: "And then: was there really betrayal on Kathryn's part? How did the king come to learn of it? Is it something that everyone at court knows about, or is it a terrible secret that I should not allude to at all? Before you leave, I beg you to hide nothing from me."

There was a bowl of apples on the table. Sir Nicholas took one, rubbed it on his sleeve and bit into it while the others waited for him to begin.

"Yes, you have the right to know. All of you, since you are all involved."

He threw the core on the fire: "You are already aware of the dubious past of the young Kathryn Howard, of her foolishness with the music teachers, of her links with Thomas Culpepper. And you know about His Majesty , so much in love. What few know is that sometime after the wedding, Kathryn had a haemorrhage. It was at night, the King was terrified. He sent for the court physician, the faithful Doctor Butts, and while he was examining the girl, Henry sat in the hallway, his back against a marble pillar, in the cold, like any other poor fellow.

'Has she had a miscarriage?' he asked, when the doctor came out of the room.

'No, Sire,' replied the doctor. He hesitated, lowered his eyes.

King Henry grabbed him by the cassock, 'Tell me!' he commanded.

So Doctor Butts reached inside his bag of instruments, took out a little bundle of white cloth and opened it, revealing a white, highly polished pebble from the riverbed. He sighed. 'It's a trick used by country people, in order to avoid pregnancy.'

The King raised his fists at him: 'You are mistaken, it is impossible.'

Butts shook his head: 'I am not mistaken.'

'Has it been there a long time?'

'Several years.'

'I am certain that my Kathryn knew nothing about it. Perhaps the old duchess had it done, when she was a baby, so as to avoid any risk when she grew up.

The doctor shut the bag of instruments: 'Her Majesty does not know that I have removed it. She will continue to bleed for several days, but she is strong, and now will be able to conceive.'

The man left, distressed, and the sovereign went in to embrace his little 'rose without thorns'."

Sad words, those of Sir Nicholas, that confirmed what the sovereign had revealed to Sir Robert, and made them aware of the tragedy that was unfolding within those walls. A deep sense of desolation oppressed them all.

"What happened to that Joan Bulmer, the friend of Kathryn's youth, who had threatened her when she had become queen?" asked Lady Constance eventually.

"Kathryn was kind, as well as naive," said Sir Nicholas, "and received her at court. The woman demanded all kinds of favours and then, when the affair with Culpepper became known, gave evidence against her. However, she was an embarrassing witness, she knew too much, so they decided to send her to rot in a dungeon somewhere in the kingdom, on charges of heresy."

In the heavy silence which fell among them, each one followed their own thoughts.

Margery: 'Poor Kathryn, a wretched orphan, no-one to wish her well.'

And Lady Constance: 'An unfortunate who sought love where she could find it.'

Sir Nicholas, on the contrary: 'A greedy little harlot, who took advantage of the sovereign's good will.'

And Sir Robert: 'How I should like to understand her better. Whether after marriage to the king she had tried to change her way of life. If that Culpepper had blackmailed her or it was she who was in search of romance.'

Philip, then, who was not yet married and whose notions of love were still unsullied: 'So young and, they say, so beautiful.'

"It happened last year."

London, Whitehall

After the pause which followed these thoughts, Sir Nicholas continued: "It all came to a head last year, in late summer. Archbishop Cranmer's spies discovered something that would incriminate Kathryn, and her uncle, the Duke of Norfolk, requested a meeting with her in private. The conversation took place in the Queen's rooms, with Cranmer and the Lord Chancellor, Thomas Audley, present too. 'Read this letter, aloud,' Norfolk instructed, handing her an unfolded sheet of paper. She, white-faced, hands shaking, cast a desperate glance at Cranmer and Audley. She had no choice but to read it. The letter that Norfolk showed me was so short that I can recite it from memory. She had written it herself to her lover while with His Majesty on a state visit to Yorkshire. It ran:

Master Culpepper, I have heard that you were ill and I have never wanted anything so much as to see you, which I hope will be soon. Come to me when Lady Rochford is here, because it will be easier for us to be together. I wish that you were here to witness the great effort that it costs me to write. Yours as long as life lasts, Kathryn

The sky had brightened, the clouds had faded away and a pale rosy light entered the room. Now the candle-flames could no longer be discerned reflected in the windows. Margery got up to extinguish some of them.

"For economy's sake," she exclaimed, provoking a smile from everyone.

Sir Robert's voice seemed to come from a long way away when he asked, in a whisper: "How did the King get to find out about it?"

"This was the dilemma," replied Sir Nicholas. "Everyone knew about Kathryn's love affair, from His Majesty's gentlemen to his stable hands, from the Queen's ladies-in-waiting to the palace washerwomen. Not him, in love like a youth, his heart couldn't have borne it. And then, who would have the courage to tell him the truth?"

"And yet, on the other hand," murmured Sir Robert, "if the woman had become pregnant, how could Culpepper's bastard be allowed to succeed to the throne of England..."

Sir Nicholas resumed the narrative, while the others listened with a growing sense of bewilderment: "To appraise the sovereign of the facts, Archbishop Cranmer decided that it would be best to write him a letter and refer to specific people – her presumed lovers, Henry Manox, Francis Dereham, Thomas Culpepper – , and to particular places where events could be verified: Horsham, Lambeth Palace, Pontefract. He had it left in church by a servant, on the prie-dieu during morning mass.

"It happened in London?" asked Lady Constance.

"At Hampton Court. The prayers over, King Henry kissed Kathryn's hand devotedly, 'You look like a Madonna,' he told her. He picked up the letter, thinking it a petition, went with Cranmer into his study, where he had some papers to sign."

"And when he opened it..." pursued Lady Constance.

"He seized Cranmer by the neck – it was the Archbishop himself who told me this. 'Why have you done this to me?' he said, with bloodshot eyes.'

"And Cranmer?"

"He replied that he had interrogated all kinds of witnesses – the chambermaids, Francis Dereham, who had been her lover for a year and had wanted to marry her, and Thomas Culpepper, the current lover. Not just relations before the royal marriage, then, but adultery, afterwards, at the expense of the King's person. He showed the sovereign Kathryn's letter to Culpepper – they found it when searching his room. The proof was indisputable.

"What became of Culpepper?"

London, Whitehall

So Henry recalled the time at Oatlands, Kathryn's bedroom door barred against him on his return from London, Lady Rochford, who had kept him back, the night of the haemorrhage – and he who had hoped for a pregnancy. The girl's self-possession on the first wedding night...

He started to cry, and sobbed leaning on the Archbishop, who put an arm around his shoulders. When he had recovered himself, he gave orders that steps be taken, without regard for anyone.

Suddenly the fire collapsed and an ember fell against the fire-guard.

"What became of Culpepper?" asked Margery.

"Arrested, tortured in the Tower with red-hot irons, his nails pulled out, the spiked collar which pierced his neck. At the end he cried out 'I didn't want to, but she kept on pestering me!' They tried him in the Great Hall of the Tower, where Anne Boleyn's trial had taken place."

"And...?"

"Pronounced guilty of having had carnal relations with the sovereign's wife, he met a traitor's death. He was taken in chains from the Tower to the gallows at Tyburn and hung

there, taken down while still alive, then drawn and
quartered, his head stuck on a pike and displayed on
London Bridge. This happened last year, in December."
"And Queen Kathryn?" asked Lady Constance.
"Her last meeting with the King was dramatic. Chancellor
Audley recounted to me how the King burst into the young
woman's room calling her a harlot. He had a dagger in his
hand, she thought that he meant to kill her and threw
herself at his feet. 'I so wanted to become Queen, if I had
told you everything, you would not have married me.
But I did swear to be faithful to you,' she wailed.
'And how long did your oath last?'
'He blackmailed me, I was frightened.'
'And the letter? To me you have never written a word.'
'I find it hard to write.'
'There you say that you love him. You came to bed with me
and wanted him. Whore! Whore first, and then adulteress!
And stupid, too. Your cousin Anne was also depraved, but
at least she was intelligent!'

If only she hadn't lied, Henry shouted, if she had told him
the truth immediately. But no: falsehood, trickery. Mockery.
She had to pay with her life – but he knew that his own
youth would die with her, leaving him nothing but the
bleakness of old age.
Kathryn expected the King to plunge the dagger in her
breast, so Chancellor Audley told me: he had it drawn and
was staggering towards her when he and Cranmer burst
into the room with some soldiers. Cranmer took hold of his
arm, Audley slid the dagger out of his hand. 'Come. Sire,'
they said to him, 'It's not worth it.' He allowed himself to
be led away.

Sir Nicholas rose, rested his hands on the mantelpiece, stared into the fire for a good while: "It was I who went to arrest her, together with Norfolk. It happened unexpectedly, Norfolk had had his orders from the sovereign only moments before."

"Where was she?" enquired Sir Robert.

"At Hampton Court, in her rooms."

"What were the orders?"

"Norfolk told me: 'We shall enter the queen's rooms. We shall seal and remove her trunks, her cases, her caskets. We shall leave her four women, we shall dismiss the rest.'"

"Then what happened?"

"It was clear that the young queen did not recognize the gravity of the situation: her ladies were trying new steps with a dancing master and she was in the window seat watching when we arrived. 'The time for dancing is over,' Norfolk announced. He treated her as if she had not been his niece. I had the orders executed while she begged to know the reason. 'I can tell you nothing, except that the king does not wish to see you until your position has been clarified,' said Norfolk. At those words she started crying, it was painful to behold."

"Did you see her again?"

"The court issued a decree against her, and I had to deliver the document to her. It stated that she would be tried 'for having led am abhorrent life, as a common whore prior to marriage, and even after, under a show of chastity and virtue, so that the sovereign's children would have been bastards.' Those were the words. The decree was signed by the king."

The silence in the room had become such that there could be heard the running of the river and the whispering of the breeze among the trees in the palace gardens.

"Tell us what happened next," prompted Sir Robert.

"When she realized what was happening, she slipped our guard and ran along the corridor towards the chapel with the star-studded blue ceiling, where she knew she would find the King at prayer. She was sure that he still loved her. 'Henry, I beg you, forgive me!' she screamed, and hammered desperately at the door. He did not come out. They were obliged to drag her away."

"Cecily told me that at night they hear the sound of footsteps along that same corridor, and the cries and groans of a young woman," murmured Margery.

"And you, where did you take her?" asked Sir Robert finally.

"We transferred her to Brentford, to the old guest-house of Syon Abbey. She was allowed to take with her some head-pieces, six velvet dresses from which the precious stones had been removed, and two fur-lined cloaks. We consigned her caskets of jewels to the King's Treasurer. She is still at Brentford now. The trial will take place in a few days' time. And then we shall know."

Sarah

London, Whitehall

In the afternoon that same day, as Sir Robert was sorting some papers prior to beginning his interrogations, a servant arrived with a document. He scanned it, shook his head, said: "Listen, it's from the Guild of Physicians and Apothecaries. In reply to my request for information regarding Joseph Godfrey, they write that 'the king's physician is one whose conduct is above suspicion.'
As you can see, another blank. But it was well and truly suspicious that fall of his sister's down the stairs…"

Just at that moment a guard showed in Sarah Godfrey, the merchant's widow, to be questioned.
The difference between her and her father was striking, Sarah was slim and elegant in her figure. She had beautiful dark hair which stood out against the pale-green of her dress, the neck slender, the face melancholic with high eye-brows and retaining a girlish shyness.
She halted on the threshold, bowed slightly: "Gentlemen."
'What a mysterious thing is charm,' thought Sir Robert when he saw her. 'A single word, a look, and we are all captivated by her.'

But when he saw that his wife was observing him with an imperceptible smile on her lips, he hastened to don his small round spectacles which conferred on him the appearance of a wise owl, and to assume a professional air.

Philip bade the young woman take the seat facing the table, Sir Robert drew a sheet from a leather folder, read some lines from it and raised his eyes towards her: "Sarah Godfrey, married name Tiler, wife of the deceased Matthew Tiler?"

"Yes, sir."

"Tell me about yourself."

She hesitated: "What should I tell you?"

"About where you come from. About your family. About how you live, the things you do."

Sarah gathered her cloak about herself.

"Are you cold?" asked Sir Robert.

"No, it's just that..."

She raised her head, looked him in the eyes: "Sir," she began, "our family comes from Spain – we too are fugitives, as Jews have always been. When there was the great plague on the Continent, that 'Black Death' brought by ships from the East, we were everywhere persecuted, massacred, burnt alive together with our manuscripts. Since few of us died of that pestilence we were accused of witchcraft, they said we were poisoning the wells in order to spread the disease."

"But it is true that the plague struck you less frequently than others," objected Sir Nicholas.

"Our communities lived together in particular districts of cities and we followed strict religious practices with respect to household cleanliness and in the preparation of food."

In contrast to her father, Sarah spoke in a subdued manner, her voice was rich, caressing. She was now looking at the window and in that light her eyes acquired the softness of silk.

"I pray you, continue," Sir Robert encouraged her.

"In the years which followed, under the rulers of Castille and Aragon, our situation changed and we began to enjoy the protection of the royal court."

Sir Robert remembered reading that many Jews in that period had been diplomats, doctors, astronomers, and many the translators of the scientific treatises in Arabic that he himself had studied.

"But when the Inquisition became more powerful and forced conversion to the Christian faith," continued the woman, "my grandfather decided to flee and seek refuge here, in London, where he had friends. He recounted to me how a group of them embarked at a cove near the port of La Coruña: in the dark a Cornish smugglers' boat was awaiting them."

She seemed to think: "He told me of how many perished in storms and were lost at sea, and that he and his family lived in poverty in London. But gradually his reputation as a healer spread, so he was secretly called to treat Henry VII Tudor, the father of our present sovereign."

"Who died spitting blood," commented ironically Sir Nicholas.

"It was too late for my grandfather to save him, though he certainly reduced his suffering. My father was born here, and became the medical astrologist that you have met, my mother died in giving birth to me, it was my father who raised me."

She smiled: "They say that is why I am a little wild."

"Your father is an astrologist. But aren't Jews forbidden to practise astrology?" retorted Sir Nicholas.

"It is forbidden to forecast the future, but not to discover the messages which the stars offer us. In the Torah it is written that 'God led Abraham into the open and said to him: Observe the night-sky and count the stars. As numberless as these shall be your descendants.' "

"And you, do you read the stars?" asked Sir Robert.

"That is my father's business. He has taught me instead to hunt for roots and leaves which cure."

"How do you search for them?"

"There are special days, or at night certain phases of the moon. Then I gather mandrake to treat sterility, betony for catarrh, valerian to induce sleep."

"These are witches' secrets!" exclaimed Sir Nicholas.

"No, sir, apothecaries have always known about such matters."

Sir Nicholas rose and took some steps towards the ladies: "I have to leave London in a few days and she is wasting our time with her stories."

And he turned to Sir Robert: "What will you tell the king? About the sufferings of the Jews? About their herbal remedies? She should, instead, talk to us about the dead man. About his will. She should explain to us why she was not at court on the evening of the murder. And of how a woman who collects herbs can be intimate with a queen."

Sarah did not allow herself to be intimidated. "Ask me what you wish about my late husband, I shall tell you everything that I know. His will? He drafted it last January, he read it to me, he left me some valuable pearls — he was always good to me. That evening I wasn't at the court banquet because I didn't feel well."

"What about the queen, then?" asked Sir Nicholas.

"As for the queen, she had had a haemorrhage, she was bleeding: she was in great pain. My father was treating the king at that time and I assisted him in this. That was how she came to send for me, secretly, with a certain Joan

Bulmer, one of her ladies, as a go-between. It was night-time, she was as white as the paper you are writing on, sir, she was suffering a lot. I felt sorry for her. I helped her by applying an ointment made up on a base of equisetum to stop the bleeding, with aloe for healing, and with a concentrated extract of valerian to dull the pain."

"Very good," confirmed Sir Robert.

"I stayed to watch over her the whole night and visited her again in the following days. I realized that she was very lonely, that she was not happy, that she had never been, that she loved someone else, not the King. I could sympathize with her. So when she asked me to be her friend, I was very happy. As for the rest of her affairs, of how Joan Bulmer was arrested and then disappeared with nothing more being heard of her: you certainly know more than I."

The final words were uttered with weariness, the woman was ashen-faced, her forehead bathed in sweat, and she had grasped hold of the edge of the table as if she felt the room spinning round. Lady Constance approached her from the shadows where she had retired and lightly touched her shoulder with her hand: for an instant the two women looked each other in the eye and one glance sufficed to establish a mutual understanding.

"Robert, do you not see that Mistress Tiler is not well? Let her go, you can just as well carry on tomorrow."

Margery too had drawn near. While Philip helped the young woman to rise, she put an arm around her waist: "Come on, up you get, my child," then slowly she led her out.

Sir Robert was taken aback. "But Constance..." he tried to protest.

"No buts! It really is true that men understand nothing. Haven't you noticed her hesitation when walking? Her exhaustion, the way she keeps pulling her cloak over her front? Haven't you realized that the woman is expecting a baby?"

A posthumous accusation

London, Whitehall

The morning after, as Sir Robert, Lady Constance, Philip
and Margery, closely wrapped in their cloaks were taking
their usual walk in the palace gardens, an attendant from
the Court of Justice approached them: "Sir Robert
Kytchyn? I have been instructed to deliver this letter to
you."
Sir Robert gave him a coin, broke the glossy red seal,
glanced at the document: "I don't have my spectacles with
me," he said, and passed it to Philip, who read:

From the Ecclesiastical Court of Justice in London

To His Honour Sir Robert Kytchyn
Palace of Whitehall

Your Honour
Among the papers removed from the house of the
merchant Matthew Tiler and consigned to this Court of
Justice, there has been found a statement signed by Esther

"I can't believe it!" exclaimed Lady Constance.

"It's absurd!" added Margery.

And Sir Robert: "I pray you, Philip, go and find Sir Nicholas and have him read the letter, tell him that we await him in our rooms."

After a short while Sir Nicholas joined them, clearly pleased: "I was right, everything about her suggested it. The story of the Jews to win our sympathy, the fact that she is friend of a queen who is little better than a prostitute..."

Sir Nicholas soon had in hand a warrant from the Court of Justice and together with Sir Robert, Philip and some guards went for a second time to the merchant's house.

The house appeared deserted, the shutters closed, no-one to answer the door.

"Let us go round the back," ordered Sir Nicholas.

They found a small garden covered in snow, pushed open the coarse wooden door, crossed a tiny dark kitchen and found themselves in the downstairs sitting-room.

Sir Nicholas explained to the guards: "We must find a document hidden somewhere in this room," and he himself started tapping with the hilt of his dagger on the walls surrounding the fireplace, where there was often a hollow brick used as a hiding-place.

Sir Robert occupied himself in sifting through the books on the shelves: some precious manuscripts on parchment and large tomes bound in brown leather. With a scholar's care he opened one of these, the thick pages worn at the edges and yellow with age: however, he could not read it as the writing was in Aramaic. He looked among note-books, astral charts, a number of diaries bound in cloth, and was struck with admiration at the doctor's learning, so far ahead of its time. But, like Sir Nicholas, he found no will hidden among the papers.

While they were rummaging around, Godfrey appeared at the doorway: "What ever..."

Sir Nicholas showed him the warrant, he in turn murmured: "Perhaps in the corner of the hearth, under the mat."

"We've already looked. There's nothing there," said a soldier.

"There's double flooring next to the staircase, and underneath a small drawer. My son-in-law kept money there."

They pulled out the small box, opened it, and at that moment Sarah arrived too. The woman halted on the doorstep and looked around in bewilderment.

In the box there was no money, only a few papers, and among them was a sheet folded in four. Sir Nicholas opened it and read aloud:

> *'In the name of God, Amen. The tenth day of January 1542, in the reign of King Henry VIII of England, I, Matthew Tiler, being of sound mind and memory, declare and record my testament as follows:*
> *I leave to my legitimate spouse Sarah all that is mine, money and property, without exception, and with this I abrogate any other previous wills. Below is a list of my goods.*
> *Written in London on the day and in the year cited above.'*

They all turned towards Sarah, and Sir Nicholas showed her the paper: "Here we are. Written two days before he was murdered."

Unsettled, the woman looked around: "But sir, I..."

"It is proof that you killed your poor husband!"

"It cannot be. I..."

"Be quiet!" ordered Sir Nicholas.

He tapped his fingers on the document, turned to Sir Robert: "This is the evidence I was searching for, nothing more is needed. Since the Ecclesiastical Court will be involved in the case, I'll have her taken to the Clink prison to await trial."

Sarah cast an anxious look towards her father, who remained mute, motionless. She wondered if she should try to exculpate herself, explain, but the fact that he did not defend her suggested he was guilty of something. She chose to remain silent. She went upstairs to put some clothes and her medicines in a bag, and left with the guards.

"Treat her with respect," Sir Robert told them.

But no respect was shown.

"There's some intrigue behind this."

London, Whitehall

When they returned to Whitehall, Sir Robert revealed to Lady Constance and Margery what had happened. The two women were shocked: "It's not possible. We have heard only good things about her. One who treats the poor as she would the king."

"There's some intrigue behind this," affirmed Margery decidedly.

"I too am perplexed," said Sir Robert. "Too swift the whole thing, and no real proof, only an accusation. And by whom, then? By someone who detested her. What is more, I saw Norfolk talking with two women, and when Sarah came out into the street they spat curses at her. 'You're for the gallows,' the older one had bawled at her. I learned later that the woman was among those whom Sarah had treated for scabies, for free."

"Old witches," pronounced Margery again.

And Sir Robert: "The sovereign insisted that the case be closed as soon as possible. Nicholas is to leave London in days and has seized this opportunity. Even now he is with the king, giving his report."

"And Henry will be satisfied, what does he care if the girl is innocent or not," added Lady Constance.

"But in fact, ladies, how can you be sure? And then, Connie, it was you who said she was expecting a baby: could it be the child of that old man? Won't there be a lover somewhere?"

"Even though the baby was another's, perhaps of someone as young as herself? Do you recall Sarah's words? 'I realized that Queen Kathryn was very lonely, that she wasn't happy, that she had never been so, that she loved another. I could understand her,' she said."

And while Margery was busy with one of her enquiries in the kitchen, Sir Robert had sunk onto the window seat, Lady Constance seated herself beside him: "Robert, does it not seem strange to you that there should suddenly appear a document which blames her so precisely? Might it not be that someone has set a trap for her? Wouldn't it be the case to discover who would wish to do so?"

"That's obvious: the same person who made the accusation, that is Esther Godfrey. But why?"

"To smear her, or worse. She hated Sarah and the merchant. Indeed, might not Esther herself be implicated in some way in the killing of old Tiler? Remember the business of the fire? And how Doctor Godfrey fled in dismay when you read him the original will? Did he know of the false will? How much did he know? He rushed home and she died strangled."

"It can't be certain that he rushed home to strangle her."

"But it is possible."

A silence fell between them. Then Lady Constance asked: "Is there nothing you can do? Technically it's your investigation, not Nicholas'."

"But there's the sovereign involved. Nicholas has not told me openly, but the king's anger against Godfrey's daughter is mounting, it seems that in some way she reminds him of Anne Boleyn, 'the witch', the wife he sent to the block. So Nicholas must close the case. 'I do not wish to be a loser. No-one loves a loser, still less a king,' he said to me. So I shall be in trouble if I interfere."

"So you can do nothing more?"

"Perhaps I could continue with my enquiries into the killing as if I were following clues on a different trail. Go to the woman in the Clink, question her, seek to understand. As long as she convinces me she is innocent, I could study the case with a good lawyer: if he secured favourable witnesses, it could be pleaded that the old man died accidentally when he fell. But in any case I should have to answer to the king."

"Will you be allowed to see her?"

"All is possible with money. Listen…"

Burnt alive, like a witch

London, Whitehall, then Bishopsgate

"All is possible with money," repeated Sir Robert. At that moment Margery rushed into the room: flustered, out of breath, she collapsed on the bench in front of the fire. Lady Constance put her arms round her, then had some spiced wine warmed on the fire and gave it to her.

Sir Robert too sought to comfort her: " Do tell us…"

When finally she managed to speak, the woman gasped: "Cicely told me… there's a rumour going round the Palace… one of the soldiers who accompanied you to where the crime took place that morning… went to see a healer for a pain in the knee… she's called Sybil, lives in a little cottage just outside Bishopsgate."

"The court doctor used to speak of her," murmured Sir Robert. "Once even I went there, with him."

Lady Constance sat down beside Margery: "Do you remember, Maggie? It was for that obstinate cough of yours, that fever that would not go away."

And Sir Robert: "The woman gave me an infusion of betony and marsh mallow. For the temperature a decoction of holly, willow and ash."

"It worked," sighed Margery in a small voice.

And Sir Robert: "I have memory of a little old woman, with a few grey hairs, bent double by age."

He paused, as if to recall more clearly: "A small cottage? A red door, battered. Two shutters on the window above the workshop. Inside, amidst a tangle of alembics and a cacophony of cats, the smell of salves and infusions."

He stayed silent for a moment. Finally: "A good woman, they told me then, who gifts her potions to the poorest. But as for me, who had come in the name of the king, she made me pay for them: and how she made me pay!"

With that remark the tension evaporated. Margery continued: "This is what I wanted to tell you: that the fellow I mentioned that went there saw that on the balcony there was – can you guess? – , a dagger."

"A dagger?!" exclaimed Sir Robert.

"A stiletto."

"On the balcony?"

"Together with the other tools. Costly, the man said."

"How, costly?"

"Because of the silver hilt. And stained with blood."

Sir Robert rose abruptly, red in the face, one boot still on, the other in his hand: "By the Lord's bones, and if there were to be a link with that other stiletto? Do you remember what I said when we first saw Matthew's corpse? 'If they had been professional thieves, they would not have left behind the stiletto with which he was killed. The hilt is of engraved silver, the weapon of a gentleman.'"

He added: "If this were to be a real clue!" and started to replace his boot.

"You shall not go there alone," decreed Lady Constance. "I'll have Sir Nicholas summoned, so that he can go with you."

And while Sir Robert looked at his wife in surprise —
though he was not courageous, it would not be the first
time that he had put himself at risk by scouring the
notorious alleyways of Southgate, in search of some detail
about a death which troubled him. He repeated: "A second
stiletto, bloodstained. A conspiracy, perhaps? The Pope, the
Spanish... But what was it doing there?"
A flurry of conjectures followed:
"And what would an old woman like Sybil have to do with
a killer?"
"Someone ill that she was treating?"
"In that case Nicholas could have him followed."
"Have the workshop watched?"
"But if a friend went there for him?"
"Or a woman?"

When Sir Nicholas arrived, Sir Robert gave him the facts,
so the two friends took their horses and rode hurriedly to
Bishopsgate.
In the almost deserted alley they were met by a dense cloud
of smoke, the acrid aftermath of burning. The workshop
had been razed to the ground, the shutters a mass of
blackened embers. When they arrived, none of those
present — all local people — , said anything, no-one moved:
there was fear in their eyes.
Finally an old woman drew cautiously near to the two
gentlemen: "It was during the night," she said in a low
voice. "Done on purpose. This morning the king's watch
found the burnt body. What remained of her was kneeling,
hands clasped together as if pleading for mercy."
"Have they discovered who was responsible?"
"She was poor, what do you expect them to discover? She
was burnt alive, as they do with witches, that's all. And
that's how they thanked her for all the good that she did."

"They say that there was money in the shop, perhaps something of value," suggested Sir Nicholas. "If it was here, the watchmen will have taken it,"

She added: "You seem upset: you knew her?"

Sir Robert raised his hands, as in a gesture of resignation: "I had known her, yes. That it should all have ended like this pains me greatly."

"You can't imagine how greatly," seconded Sir Nicholas.

The two were just reaching the end of Tower Bridge when Sir Robert suddenly stopped:

"But why set fire to the workshop? The dagger... Was there some evidence that must be destroyed?"

"And why kill that poor woman?" added Sir Nicholas. "There must be something behind this."

The Clink

London, Southwark, Clink Prison

It was only on Monday that Sir Robert obtained the necessary authorization from the Ecclesiastical Court of Justice to gain access to the Clink.

The prison was next to an old priory, to the south of the river, just beyond London Bridge. It was amongst the oldest in England, though not as harsh as the one at Newgate, nor like the dungeons in the Tower: it was under the jurisdiction of the Bishop of Winchester and at that time torture was forbidden there.

Sir Robert explained to Philip, who accompanied him: "The Clink is a profitable institution: one of the reasons is that imprisoned there are prostitutes without a licence who can continue their trade, and who pay well. The warders have meagre wages but do well from the rich inmates. They let rooms with beds, sheets, candles, even a fire to those who have money."

"The Clink, why is it so called?"

"It is said to come from the clanking of the chains which they used to put on the prisoners."

Entrance to the prison was through an archway of bright red bricks, which contrasted sharply with the white of the snow in nearby orchards.

Sir Robert and Philip tied their horses to the rings in the wall, a gate-keeper with a pock-marked face and an unwelcoming expression opened the gate for them: a silver coin served to make him more agreeable.

Sir Robert introduced himself: "I am the special coroner appointed by the sovereign for the investigation into the death of the merchant Matthew Tiler," and showed his pass. "I need to see someone who was brought here last Friday, a certain Sarah Godfrey, the widow of Matthew Tiler."

"Certainly, sir, but it is a warder who will take you," and he passed them to one such who looked even less pleasant.

This man, who certainly did not know how to read, and from whose mouth with its black teeth issued a foul breath, wished to examine Sir Robert's document. He opened it upside down and pretended to read it. Sir Robert turned it round for him.

Another feigned reading, then the man asked: "Has the young man a permit too?"

Again a coin changed hands: "All in order, sir," and the three proceeded along a dark hallway.

Shiny, black cockroaches

London, Southwark, Clink Prison

The warder pointed to some cells behind a metal grill door.
"It's in those rooms that Bishop Richard Fox, now dead,
had us put the instruments of torture. They can't be used
any more. In my opinion it's a great shame that all we have
left are beatings and whippings, and bread and water in
solitary."

"Sir Robert," said Philip, "I should find it interesting to see
those instruments."

Another coin convinced the warder that yes, they could see
them and he would explain how they worked.

He opened the door and lighted the room with his torch.
"Here we are," he said revealing two metal bars with spikes,
attached to one another by screws. "These were for
crushing thumbs. The thumbs were pushed between the
bars, and the bars were tightened, like this. If the accused
talked, well and good, if not they became mush."

Then they saw a number of irons hanging on the wall:
"They are for branding: P for prostitute, F for felon,"
explained the man. "And these others are rings for the
head-splitter. You can see – and he brought them close,
pointing with a grimy finger – , here inside there are nails,

these screws tighten the ring and bit by bit the nails go into the head."

Their gaze was arrested by an iron chair, its seat set with sharp metal points: "It was called the 'Inquisition Chair', it was to make witches confess," explained the man. "They were made to sit there, no clothes on and bound fast so they couldn't stand. Then the fire was lit below, and the chair became red-hot."

He laughed, amused: "The women began to squirm, it was fun to watch. And the iron points tore their backsides and the fire burned the wounds, and you could smell burning flesh even outside."

The man smirked unpleasantly as he spoke. Sir Robert noticed that Philip looked as if he was going to be sick and was about to say: 'Let's leave,' but the warder continued:

"And see here, this is 'the stake.' A wonder: you pushed this sharp end, do you see, up the arse of the accused and made it come out by the shoulders. It took real skill. You hadn't to pierce the bowels or the heart, or else the man died at once. If he confessed he might even survive, if not it took days to die."

A crooked smile lit his face: "And it worked better still if it was done with man hanging head down."

Sir Robert grabbed Philip and dragged him out.

"I'll take you to the women's part," said the warder.

They walked along a corridor flanked by the men's cells. In these on the straw lay abandoned creatures, spindly, filthy, even though no longer in chains. Every so often the younger among them would manage to catch a rat, which was skinned and eaten on the spot. Shiny, black cockroaches ran across the floor, bed bugs and lice proliferated, damp trickled down the walls, the stench of excrement and urine was overwhelming.

"Because I don't know how to write."

London, Southwark, Clink Prison

The woman's section, beyond a second courtyard, was less sordid, but the poor wretches there begged money so they could eat, and stretched their scrawny arms through the bars which, over the centuries, had witnessed so much desperation.

Sarah was in a tiny cell, fairly clean – the prison governor had been a patient of Doctor Godfrey's. Shut in with her was an old prostitute so crippled that she could no longer practise her profession or, for that reason, pay the gaolers. Sarah was attending to her feet by applying a yellow ointment which smelt of rosemary.

"Sir Robert!" she exclaimed when she saw him, and she looked pleased. "I pray you, come and see." She explained to the woman: "This gentleman is a doctor."

Sir Robert crouched down beside the old woman, lifted the bandage, noted the swollen, blackened feet. "Gangrene," he declared. "Do you see here? The tissue is putrefied. What infection have you had?"

The woman raised towards him watery eyes in a bloated face. "Sir, how do I know? When one leads a life like mine..."

He realized that he had been foolish to put such a question. "And now?" asked Sarah.

"At this stage amputation is the only option."

The old woman had started to cry, he caressed her head. "Otherwise, one dies," he told her quietly, "and it is a painful death. I'll speak to the prison doctor, if you wish." He turned to Philip: "Re-do her bandage, please."

Then he took Sarah apart in a corner of the cell, gave her a bag containing some clean clothes, a thick woollen shawl, some marzipan sweets. "This is from my women, who are convinced of your innocence."

He brushed aside her thanks, and they sat down together on the straw.

"So, Mistress Tiler..."

"My name is Sarah."

"Sarah, I am here to learn the truth. Did you write that will?"

The woman seemed to hesitate. "I tried to say, but they wouldn't let me speak."

"Well, tell me. I pray you. If I know what really happened I may be able to do something for you."

"And if what I tell you harms someone else? Will you swear to keep it secret?"

"You are referring to who killed your husband? That is, if what you tell me will reveal the murderer?"

"I don't know who is culpable, it's only a suspicion on my part."

Sir Robert reflected. Eventually: "I can swear to you that I shall act with circumspection, and that I shall do all I can to help you."

She looked at him with her mysterious eyes, as if she could read his mind: "It was not I who wrote that document.

Because I don't know how to write, I know only to sign my name."

Now it was his turn to look into her eyes: "But you read the names of remedies, I have seen you selecting them when I was with the king."

"Those I can read in that I recognize the labels with the pictures on the jars, I've known them since I was child. And also in the book, the images help me. Or my father explained them to me."

At the thought of the father she murmured: "He didn't defend me. Why not?"

On the wall were scratched with a nail names and dates: a long job, tiring, done for others by someone who could write. Sir Robert read:

'Thomas Archer was here... Anthony Longton... Mathias 1244.' So there have been men inside here too, he thought. And then: 'Joan... Maud of Southwark... Jesus have pity...'

"Why didn't your father defend you? I don't know. Were you alluding to him when you were seeking to protect someone?"

"Not to him."

"Is it true that you are expecting a baby?"

"Yes."

"Did you love another?"

She paused: "I was fond of Matthew. But it's true, I loved someone else."

"Do you wish to tell me who?"

"I can't."

"Where is he now?"

"I don't know."

"Why is he not here to defend you? Why has he abandoned you?"

Like the old woman, Sarah now started to cry, silently, her head resting on her knees.

'Two women, two such different lives,' thought Sir Robert, 'and both weeping for themselves. For their abandonment. For a sorrow as old as the world.'

He observed the young widow, and became increasingly sure that she was innocent of her husband's murder. Perhaps she did not love him, but she respected him. And there grew within him the desire to aid her.

"Time's over, sir," said the warder opening the door. "The prison governor says that Sarah Godfrey will appear before a court this coming Friday."

Sir Robert rose, rubbed his sore back, brushed some wisps of straw from his cloak: "I shall return tomorrow, Sarah. I hope that you will feel able to tell me more."

But the following day, when he arrived at the Clink, the gate-keeper told him that the woman was no longer there.

"So where is she?" asked Sir Robert.

"I don't know."

"Has she been moved?"

"No idea."

"Didn't they tell you?"

"Me? Nobody tells me nothing. The prison governor, perhaps…"

"I shall be hanged for what I did."

London, the merchant's house

Sir Robert left the Clink prison and headed for the merchant's house in the same district. He racked his brains: vanished from the Clink, what had happened to Sarah? Killed, perhaps? And then, where had the corpse gone? Or she had fled, but how could she have done? Had someone helped her? Where had she fled? Certainly not to her father's, the first place they would look. She had to be found, and hidden from the king's henchmen until things had become calmer. And why hadn't Godfrey defended her? Why had the man not immediately revealed what he knew of the will? Why such reticence regarding his sister's death?

He found him in the kitchen, bent over the fire, engrossed in preparing an infusion.
"Here again? What more do you want from me?"
Sir Robert was not perturbed: "I have to ask you some questions. Seat yourself there."
He indicated a bench and he himself sat down on a stool:
"When I interviewed you in my study, when I read you the will, the one registered by Tiler, you ran away. Why?"

Godfrey did not reply. Curled up he kept pulling at the edge of his tunic.

"Let me tell you then. You had realized that your sister Esther was plotting some trick against Sarah. When I asked you whether you knew that Matthew Tiler had made you a beneficiary in his will you remembered something that Esther had said. You took fright, you ran home in order to get an explanation. You had to be alone with her, so you sent the servants out, you sent them well away. After all, what need was there of an apothecary in Cheapside when there was one just round the corner? The same for the beer: why did you send a servant as far as Tower Hill when Southwark teems with ale-houses?

Still Godfrey kept quiet, his eyes on the floor, his hands trembling. At last, slowly, he began to speak: "It is time to lift this weight off my chest. I know that you are a reputable man, Sir Robert. And a good doctor, I have read your treatises. However, as you will be aware, we who treat the maladies of others, are ourselves often afflicted, here inside, and we don't realize it. That is what happened to me when my wife died. We had fled Spain at night, like thieves, which we certainly weren't. We started a new life here, faithful to the Torah, to study, to work. When our baby was born, my wife Leah died. She was very beautiful my Leah, and she loved me…"

Sir Robert listened, pensively.

"Like Job I raised my fist to heaven against the Almighty: what sense has our life, I hurled, if you lie there in ambush, like an envious demon, in order to take from us those we love? And then, without knowing it, I became what I am."

In the hearth the fire was dying, the two men seemed not to notice.

"So as not to die from despair, I closed my heart to all, even to the little Sarah. To avoid being hurt again, I grew hard. Sarah became a woman without my really noticing, and then for my benefit I gave her in marriage to a man she did not love. She cried so much, I believe that she hated me for it."

"Didn't you realize that she allowed herself to be led away to prison without saying a word when she suspected that you were guilty of a crime?"

"I have realized it in these evenings of solitude. Without Matthew, without Esther, without Sarah any more, without anyone to love me."

'Without anyone to love,' thought Sir Robert.

Godfrey shivered. He revived the fire with the poker, threw on some more wood. He poured a little of the steaming mixture from the pot into two pewter beakers, added some honey and offered one to Sir Robert.

Sir Robert reflected: 'And I, what would I have become if Constance had died when our child was born? How would I have lived without her? Would I have gone out of my mind, would I have begged God that I might die?'

He decided that for the moment he would say nothing to him about Sarah's disappearance. He said instead: "I need to know more about your daughter, about yourself, about your sister Esther, about what exactly happened on that day that you ran home.."

Godfrey hesitated, took a few sips from his beaker, placed it on the mantelpiece above the fireplace. Eventually: "Well, I shall tell you about that accursed day. It is true, I ran home, sent out the servants, joined her in the room upstairs. "The king's coroner has read me Matthew Tiler's will. What is it you were muttering some evenings ago, that Sarah was greedy and unscrupulous? That you would make her fall into her own trap? She stormed at me, she was beside herself: "I have had to bear it all in these past years! From you, who took away my man! From her, whom I had raised as a daughter, who stabbed me in the back! And to have to live in this house, all together, as if nothing had happened – humiliated, scorned. You'll all pay for it, oh you shall all pay. Matthew has already paid, soon it will be Sarah's time. I have cooked her to a turn, the child!"

I sought to interrupt her fury: "What do you mean, what have you concocted against her?"

Esther's face was contorted with hatred, she cried: "She'll be dragged to court, she'll be hanged!"

I didn't know what I was doing, my sister showed herself for what she was, a repulsive woman, jealous of that youthful beauty which she had never had. I seized her by the throat, I shook her.

We were at the top of the staircase, she tried to grasp hold of the banister, she staggered and rolled down the stairs. She was dead on the bottom step when I reached her."

After a brief silence he sighed: "Report me, they'll hang me for what I did. After such horrors it will be a relief to die."

At that moment, for the first time, Sir Robert saw him through different eyes. That man had lost his woman, he had been hollow inside like a shrivelled tree. Then he thought of Constance, he saw her beside him with her calm expression, her clear voice. And, above all, alive.

He rose: "I shall not denounce you," he said. "I shall do all I can to save your daughter, and when she returns home she must find you here waiting for her. You will have a lot to tell each other, years of words unspoken. Then it will be for you to decide whether to go and be hanged – but who would it profit? – , or to spend the rest of your life helping others. Without asking anything, as your daughter did."

Godfrey's voice trembled: "She did this? I did not know," he murmured.

When Sir Robert emerged from the merchant's house he was greeted by a perfect winter day: the wind had swept away the clouds, the sky had cleared, the air was pure and fresh. He felt at peace with himself, without knowing why.
He walked towards the Thames, admired the iridescent colours of the sunset in the water, the barges which moved slowly on the river, hailed a boat to take him to the wharf at the Palace of Whitehall. That year the river had not frozen, so no fairs on the ice, no vendors of hot food nor children on skates made from barrel staves.
Asklepios, though, he would have preferred to leave in his stall: his old horse had seemed to him tired of late, and he hadn't wanted him to go out in the cold of the morning.

Requiem for a friend

London, Palace of Whitehall

That night too Sir Robert slept badly, as had happened after his meeting with the king. He tossed in his bed, tormented by oppressive dreams: a dwarf gave Asklepios something to drink from a pail and there was a smirk on his nasty face as he saw the good animal stiffen and change into a night bird. It began to rain hard, a kind of flood: the Thames rose and Asklepios slid into the water and couldn't pull himself free. He whinnied, pleading for help, but he, Sir Robert, had heavy legs and wasn't able to move. Now they were all at Cambridge, on a market day, and the horse stopped to munch on a bundle of hay which Esther Godfrey was carrying in a basket. He wanted to shout and warn him to beware, that it might be poisoned, but no sound issued from his mouth.

So, before dawn, when a servant came to wake him and urge him to hasten to the stables, he felt his heart leap into his mouth: "Asklepios. He must be unwell," he said to his wife.

He hurried down the narrow spiral staircase that led to the courtyards, went into the stables, silent at that hour except for some shuffling in the stalls, and hushed words behind a partition at the end of the passageway.

Beyond the boarding Asklepios lay on the straw, eyes closed, short of breath. Next to him was a groom and one of the royal blacksmiths. To Sir Robert's questioning look the latter responded: "He's not ill, just very old. He's not in pain, but they know, they do, when the time has come. I'll leave you with him, so he can go in peace."

Sir Robert crouched down beside the animal, called him by name, stroked his silken neck. There came to him the words of one of his old masters: 'When nothing more can be done, all that remains is to stay close by.'

He stretched out his hand, palm uppermost, so that the horse could nuzzle it and nibble his fingers as he had always been wont to do. The animal raised his head slightly and pushed it against his knees. Sir Robert's eyes filled with tears. 'I could swear that he is saying goodbye,' he thought. 'But he mustn't see me cry.'

And with a calm voice he began speaking to him, as if he were telling a bedtime story to a child.

"Do you remember, Asklepios? It was that morning that my tutor invited me to accompany him to the horse fair at St Ives. He told me that he had to purchase another mount for himself, that he wished to make me a gift as I had been his best pupil and soon he would be sending me to practise medicine in France. I could not believe it when he took me to the colts' pen and asked me to choose one: I had never had anything of my own, and then a horse. He was fond of me, Sir Henry."

Sir Robert sighed at the memory. In a soft voice he continued: "In the pen there were lots of colts and all — don't be offended — , were more handsome than you: taller, more slender, with flowing manes. You in contrast were rather stout, and on your neck you had a few bristly hairs. But you rushed to the railings, pushed out your neck towards me, gazed at me with such trusting eyes, and with your muzzle gave me a thump on the shoulders. 'I choose him,' I said.

So Sir Henry paid, in truth but little, for you. He bought himself a horse and saddles and we returned home at a light trot, along tracks which wound through countryside green with grass and yellow with flowers. I was happy.

"What will you call him?" asked Sir Henry, touched by my obvious pleasure.

"Asklepios?" I ventured.

"It's a good name for a doctor's horse," he agreed.

Sir Robert's voice broke, but Asklepios nudged his hand with his muzzle, as if pressing him to continue.

He began again: "So we have grown up together. You, small and sturdy, greedy, as affectionate as a child, but also strong and wise. Do your remember when I presented Constance to you: I said: "We are to be married." You gave a neigh of approval and always neighed with joy when you saw her. And you had learned to roll in the grass: if I was sad, you would caper around, then you would come to lick my hand and I went away comforted. My friend..."

As Sir Robert spoke to him and stroked his muzzle and neck, the animal opened his soft eyes for a moment, gazed at him, gave a brief shudder, as if he wished to say something – and moved no more.

Later, when Lady Constance joined her husband in the stables she found him seated on a stool, weeping, his face between his hands. She hugged him, and led him out.

Morning had come, the bells were ringing the Third Hour. "I too loved him," she murmured.

Sir Barnaby

From London to Scotland

In the days which immediately followed the death of Matthew Tiler, there had been whispers in the city about a supposed relationship between a Gentleman of the Royal Bedchamber, Sir Barnaby Lowell, and Sarah, the young wife of the murdered merchant. It might have proved a fruitful line of enquiry, so Sir Robert had again raised the matter with his friend Sir Nicholas: "Gossip, I've already told you," Sir Nicholas had replied. "The two, for different reasons, frequented the court, at some reception or other the two will have been seen together. But we know now that the woman killed out of greed for money."

The case was closed. Twenty-three January, six days after the crime, Sir Barnaby had had to leave London for the North with the Duke of Norfolk, to defend the English border against the Scots. At the end of January, two weeks after the merchant's death, no-one in the city bothered about him or about his dawn departure in the depths of winter.

Indeed, in the days in which Barnaby journeyed out of London, the roads of England were frozen, the carts stuck in the snow, the wheels had to be lifted clear by hand, the horses kept slipping, and before nightfall they had to stop because a louring fog had risen from the fields and made further progress impossible. So the Duke of Norfolk's soldiers erected their white tents and warmed themselves by the fires on which they cooked their meals. Since the folk of the villages through which they passed were exhausted by the long winter and by famine, Sir Barnaby and his men often shared their rations with the poor creatures.

In such a manner, in its journey northwards, the army crossed increasingly cold counties, from Leicestershire to Nottinghamshire to Northumberland, arriving finally at Berwick-on-Tweed and its grey-stone castle on the border with Scotland.

Berwick Castle: that ancient Anglo-Saxon stronghold on the River Tweed, over the centuries contested by England and Scotland, burnt to the ground a hundred times by both parties, rebuilt, lost, reconquered.

On one of those freezing days Sir Barnaby was in his tent, a blanket over his shoulders, the brazier burning. He was absorbed in writing a letter by the light of the lantern which he held close to the paper, when a knight accompanied by a squire bearing the arms of the Lord of Carlisle arrived at the encampment below the walls of the castle. The Scottish invasion had been repulsed, much blood spilt, many atrocities committed: 'I shall never accustom myself to this slaughter,' the young Barnaby wrote to his sister. And while he sent his own news, he in turn asked a lot from her: insistently, as if stuck there in the misty North, he was desperate to know what was happening in London. As if something – a worry, a regret – , was tormenting him, making him anxious to return there.

Sir Daniel Shipwith, a messenger just arrived from London to the campfire under the castle walls, delivered some papers to the Duke of Norfolk, then entered Sir Barnaby's tent. The two, childhood friends, had virtually lost touch with each other when Sir Daniel – a powerfully-built young man, a descendant of mariners, an aquiline nose, thick chestnut eyebrows, dark eyes and a jovial manner – , was sent to Wales. They were now sitting together drinking beer by the brazier and Sir Barnaby began asking news of the capital, directing the exchange, as if carelessly, towards Southwark: "And life in the borough?"

"Same as always. Taverns full despite the lack of money. Sailors and prostitutes. Every so often some-one is killed. Were you in London when the merchant Matthew Tiler was murdered?"

"Do you know anything about it? Have they found the murderer?"

"They have arrested the merchant's wife, that Sarah the daughter of the astrologist, the one who gives herbal cures. She's been shut in the Clink."

Sir Barnaby's eyes opened wide, he tried to speak, the words stuck in his throat.

He stammered: "She's in prison? Why is that?!"

Sir Daniel looked at him in astonishment: why was his friend so affected by the news? He replied, warily: "They say she's involved in her husband's death."

"Impossible!" exclaimed Sir Barnaby. "It was Sir Robert Kytchyn who was charged by the king with the investigation of the case. James accompanied him to the scene of the crime the morning after it had happened. He could not have done this to her."

"What do we know about it? Moreover, they say the woman is expecting a child, and it's certainly not the old man's."

At these words Sir Barnaby, grown suddenly ashen-faced, leapt to his feet, stumbled over his stool and made as if to go outside.

"Do you feel ill?" Sir Daniel asked holding him back by the arm.

"I must return to London!"

"Will Norfolk allow it?"

"I am not indispensable here."

"But why, in God's name, return to London?"

"Sarah is the woman I love. If she is expecting a baby, it is mine. She hasn't killed anyone, not her. And she'll be hanged, don't you realize? She'll be hanged if I don't arrive in time."

Sir Barnaby's speech was garbled, the meaning unclear. Sir Daniel understood little of it. But he said to his friend: "I shall come with you. Norfolk will give us a pass and a priority order for the change of horses. We shall return to London together, this very night."

Sir James, his lifelong friend, having entered the tent at that moment, and knowing about Sarah, embraced Barnaby: "Good luck, my friend, may heaven protect you."

And as the two went out into the night, he murmured to himself: 'It won't be easy.'

Searching for Sarah

London, Whitehall

Later on that February morning, Sir Barnaby Lowell and Sir Daniel Shipwith reached London from the North in a storm of rain and snow. They headed straight for the Clink, and they too were told that Sarah was no longer there, that she had perhaps fled.

It was then that Sir Barnaby, devastated, hurried to Sir Robert in Whitehall. He revealed to him that Sarah, the old merchant's wife, was the woman he loved, recounted how he had met her. It had been two years before, when he had gone hunting with Sir Nicholas in Epping Forest. It had grown late, the moon had risen, the men heard a woman's cry: "Halt! Quiet!" Sir Nicholas had ordered.

They had approached, had seen a horse crushed by a tree trunk which had fallen across the path. The animal's back legs were both broken, they had had to end its suffering. The woman dragged down by the fall was Sarah Godfrey, the wife of the dead merchant, and Sir Nicholas already knew her as the assistant of the king's doctor, Joseph Godfrey. Miraculously unharmed. Sir Nicholas entrusted her to Sir Barnaby in order for him to take her back to

London on his own horse, she and the basketful of herbs she had collected in the forest.

That night the woman had leant on him trustingly, her face close to his – young like him, tender, sweet. Few words were spoken: they had fallen in love.

While Sir Barnaby remained seated by the fire, hunched over like an empty sack, Sir Robert stayed silent for a long while. He offered him some wine to drink and told him of the latest happenings with regard to Sarah.

He wondered aloud: "So our duties now are twofold: to investigate the crime and to trace her," he said. "A young woman, beautiful, penniless, in a city overflowing with riff-raff. An innocent already condemned by the sovereign. We must move quickly, before some scoundrel takes advantage of her, or the king's henchmen find her and deliver her to the hangman."

He added: "We shall have to act cautiously, no-one must know that we are searching for her. We shall put it around that we have need of someone practised in medicine, or a midwife, or perhaps a housemaid."

He had his wife and Margery summoned, and informed them of what had happened, leaving out nothing.

"From the start I was sure that Sarah wasn't guilty," affirmed Lady Constance.

"Poor boy," said Margery addressing Sir Barnaby. "And now what shall we do?"

"Try to find her," implored Sir Barnaby.

They looked at each other and were all in agreement.

"We shall share the tasks."

London, Whitehall and Southwark

"We shall share the tasks," said Sir Robert after they had all lunched together, Sir Barnaby and Sir Daniel included. "I shall return to the Clink. I must know how she managed to escape, or whether there is something else going on in that awful place."

Sir Barnaby grew pale: "What do you mean?"

The others looked at each other and said nothing.

"Someone might have bribed a guard," suggested Lady Constance in order to relieve the tension.

"In whose interest would it be to have her leave prison? Certainly not her father's, from what you told us."

The young man thought for a few moments: "Agnes, the girl from the Southwark brothel!" he exclaimed. "I know that Sarah had treated her, she might have gone to her to seek refuge."

And he rushed out before anyone could speak.

"What did you mean when you said 'I must know if there is something else going on in that awful place'?" asked Lady Constance.

"I meant the worst thing for a woman."

"Holy Virgin, no!" cried Margery.

And proposed: "Sir Robert, Cecily the cook might have heard something at the market this morning. If I were to go to her and tell her that I need Sarah for the pains in my feet – which is a fact?"

"A good idea, do it at once."

To put herself in her role, Margery left the room limping.

"And you, Sir Daniel, are you with us?" continued Sir Robert.

"With all my heart."

"Then I would ask you to visit the borough taverns: she could have gone into hiding in one of those, offering herself as a servant. Everyone is fond of her."

"Right. It will be no sacrifice to drink a few more beers."

"And me, what can I do?" asked Philip.

"For you the inns. It's likely that Sarah treated some travellers there, and so they will all know her. It's possible that she's working in one, perhaps in the kitchens."

Philip looked anxious: "I don't know London. "If I have need, will you help me?" he asked Sir Daniel.

"I'll give you a list of inns, and on the first few occasions I shall accompany you," the latter assured him.

"Robert, I can go into the parish churches," proposed Lady Constance.

"And into the small priories, those that still exist," replied Sir Robert. "Speed is of the essence, you'll go with Margery. After the Clink I shall do a tour of the London hospitals. It makes sense to begin our enquiries in Southwark, and then extend our search as far as the city gates."

"It's unlikely that she's gone beyond the city walls," observed Sir Daniel.

He added: "The gates close with the curfew bell, and at this time of year it goes dark early."

"Where's Sarah Godfrey?!"

London, Southwark

The day had started with rain and snow, now the weather had changed for the better, in the air a hint of Spring. At a very early hour Sir Robert was again at the gate of the Clink. He was met by the same gate-keeper as before: having in mind the silver coin, the latter gave a deep bow.

"I must speak with the prison governor," said Sir Robert.

"That's not possible just now, but come with me."

He accompanied him along a corridor half underground to a room with an iron grating on the windows through which could be seen the feet of passers-by. A small damp space, poorly lit by a few tallow candles. There, a man wearing the uniform of the royal guard sat with his legs stretched out by a brazier. He appeared exhausted, beneath the open collar of his shirt could be discerned a scrawny neck.

"Sir Robert Kytchyn, the coroner appointed by the king," announced the keeper.

The governor stood up hurriedly, buttoned his shirt, and offered Sir Robert a stool. "I was told that you have been here before."

"The sovereign has charged me with investigating the death of the merchant Mathew Tiler, and the person that I visited is his wife."

"Sarah Tiler née Godfrey.

"Do you know her?"

"She came to the prison on several occasions to treat sick women. When my wife was giving birth, she was here day and night. I owe it to her that she's still alive."

Sir Robert reflected: 'Will he know that Sarah is no longer in her cell? It's best that I make him talk.'

The man went to open the door of his den, looked out to right and left, came back and sat down.

"You have to be careful, these days even the stones have ears. Tell me: what is it you want of me?"

"Do you know about Sarah Godfrey?"

The man shot a nervous glance at him.

"Look..."

"Where 's Sarah Godfrey?"

"I don't know whether..."

Sir Robert, who was smaller than him, but more solidly built and above all very annoyed, grabbed him by the collar of his cassock: "Where is Sarah Godfrey?!" he shouted.

The other collapsed on the chair, his forehead bathed in sweat. "Very well," he sighed. Yes, it's better that I tell you everything."

He hesitated for some moments, finally: "I knew that Mistress Tiler was in the Clink, I had entered her name in the register myself when they brought her here. I had pretended not to know her, but in the evening I went to visit her with my wife. She was taking care of her cell-mate. My wife and Sarah embraced each other, both were crying, you know how women are made, the happier they are, the more they cry."

"True," agreed Sir Robert.

"I asked her why she was there. She replied that she didn't really know, that they were taking her to court, that there was a will involved, that when the soldiers had led her out onto the street, some women had cried out that she was witch."

'Old hags, as Margery says,' thought Sir Robert.

"Then she let on to my wife that she was expecting a baby. So Margaret, that's my wife, tore into me as if I was a worm: 'And you have the nerve to keep her in this disgusting place?' They talked together for a bit, those two, and at the end my wife said: 'Sarah knows somewhere to go, and no-one would guess she was there. They would welcome her because she knows how to treat certain kinds of people.' 'I'd be in real trouble if they found out that she's no longer here,' I replied. And my wife: 'You could always say that she's dead. Nobody would question it, with all the squalor that there is here.'"

"And you?"

"I gave in — what else could I do, against two women. Late at night I took her to the main gate. I gave her some money and Margaret put her cloak around her shoulders. I made her pull down the hood of the cloak so that no-one would recognize her."

The man halted briefly. Then: "I put my arm around her shoulders: if anyone had seen us, I would have told them that she was my wife, that she wasn't feeling well, that I was taking her to see a nurse. We didn't meet anyone and the guard was sleeping, drunk as usual."

"And you sent her out into the night alone?"

"I have a servant, a poor idiot — big and tall — , who's been with me since he was a child. I had him go with her."

"So he knows where she's gone?"

"The morning after, he didn't even remember having been out."

St Saviour's Church

London, Whitehall, and Southwark

On her return from visiting Cecily, Margery reported that she had learned nothing fresh about Sarah: "I told her that I needed Sarah Godfrey's medicines for the pains in my hands and feet, she informed me that the woman had been sent to the Clink, and nothing more. 'Is it known why?' I asked. 'It is said that she's involved in her husband's death, but I know her well, and I don't believe it,' she replied."

So Lady Constance and Margery commenced their investigation of the London churches. It would be a sad affair: after Henry VIII's break with Rome, bands of Cromwell's soldiers had sacked churches and convents, raped nuns and made human torches out of priests and friars, stolen gold chalices and crucifixes, burnt whole libraries – with the sheets of the manuscripts that rabble had wiped their boots, lit fires, cleaned their cauldrons.

The survivors of this carnage now lived on people's charity, clergy that continued in the parish churches were those who had submitted to the sovereign's new order. Courtiers close to the king had gained possession of many of the buildings taken from the church to convert them into private houses; others, of little value, were now used as stables or pig-sties.

The first place that the two women visited was St Saviour's Church in Southwark. The outside of the structure appeared almost intact, apart from a small side door which was partially charred. They pushed open the main door of heavy oak reinforced with diamond-shaped studs and nails, entered, and were accosted by a smell of incense and old stone, their footsteps echoing along the bare nave. They pulled their cloaks tightly about them at the sensation of damp which seemed to seep into their bones like a malaise.
"Look, the niches where the statues of saints used to stand are empty," said Margery.
"And they have white-washed the stories of their lives on the walls."
In a side chapel there remained a fresco of the crucified Jesus: it fixed them with forlorn eyes, with an air of infinite sadness.
"There's light at the end there," observed Lady Constance.
They approached and saw that the leaded stained glass of the transept with its lovely figures in red, blue and yellow had disappeared, in its place small panes of a greenish hue cast a dismal lustre.
"Those too stolen? And what will they do with them?" exclaimed Margery.

A light cough caused them to turn round: seated on a bench reading his prayers was a priest who gestured them to come near. He had white hair under a black beret, and emanated the odour of the vestry: "Women, do not be indiscreet," he urged them.
"Forgive us, father. It's just that we loved the stories of the Apostles on those windows."

"Sit here." He patted the bench with his hand. "Tell me, can I be of assistance to you?"

The two women sat down next to him: "It's a matter of someone who's ill, we are looking for a woman who could attend her," Lady Constance calmly lied.

The priest lay the prayer-book on his lap.

"Yes, I can help you. There are many women who come begging for work. Who is the patient? What does she need?"

Lady Constance shot a wicked glance at her companion, her eyes smiling: "What should I say? She's called Margery She's an old woman, rather grumpy. But good at heart."

And added: "For us it's vital that the woman knows about medicine."

"For example?"

"How to dress wounds, make ointments, be familiar with herbal medicines."

The priest shook his head: "As skilled as that, no. But if I should happen to find one, where can I reach you?"

"We are guests at..."

Then, remembering that even the priest might be an informer, she corrected herself: "It is of no matter, we ourselves shall return. Thank you, reverend father." She slipped a coin into the charity box, and with Margery hurried out.

If she had looked back she would have seen the perplexed expression on the face of the priest.

A visit to St Thomas' Hospital

London, Southwark

Having completed a tour of the churches to no result, on Friday Lady Constance and Margery went to St Thomas' Hospital, which Sir Robert would not have time to visit.

The institution took in about forty people, the old left alone and destitute, some sick, penniless pilgrims. When they entered that place of hospitality, each poor wretch was washed, deloused and furnished with bed-sheets: their clothes would be returned on their leaving, clean and mended.

An elderly woman met the two visitors: "We are here to make a donation," explained Lady Constance touching her purse.

"Thank you, we need them. There was a time when St Thomas' was maintained by the Augustinian canons, but since the break with Rome we have not received any money from the crown. Now the city mayor is threatening to make us close, the reason given that we take in women dying of the French disease. Would it be better to let them die in the streets, I ask myself?"

She showed them around the building, a square block

of two floors in grey stone with a turret at each of the four corners.

"The old hospital has been re-named after Thomas Becket, the holy archbishop killed at Canterbury. He was good to the needy. Here," the woman indicated a small room with two beds, "we care for unmarried mothers about to give birth. All that happens within these four walls must remain secret, so that these young women are not denied the opportunity for marriage."

"And the babies?"

"They are so few that survive..."

They stopped at a passage where the old were accommodated, some attendants were serving them something to eat, one was being fed. Through the windows of small yellow panes shone a faint light, in the air was the strong smell of straw pallets.

Lady Constance made the usual enquiry, the other replied: "A woman, Sarah by name, often used to come here to treat the sick. But I haven't seen her for a while."

The tavern girl

London, Southwark

The same day Sir Robert had gone back to the merchant's house. Here he had found an irritated Doctor Godfrey: "I have been to the Clink," had said Godfrey, "and the keeper threw me out." 'Your daughter has disappeared,' the man grunted. 'And we know nothing about her. We've searched all over the prison: nothing. If there's an enquiry I'm going to be the first to pay, I was on guard that night.' And he slammed the door in my face."

Godfrey scratched his unshaven chin with his finger-tips: "Why didn't you tell me anything? Perhaps you've found out something?"

Sir Robert had preferred not to give details: 'You never know,' he had thought. 'His closeness to the king, words that can slip out…'. "We are looking for her," he said. "If you have news, report directly to me. Directly, understand? It's a question of life or death. And, tell me, are you still treating the sovereign?"

"Still."

"He must not know about her disappearance. But if his spies have already reported to him, I would ask you to look displeased with your daughter, and to tell him that you do not want to know anything more about her. Otherwise he

would have some cutthroat put a knife in your ribs. And I
don't know if you have noticed: there is a guard in front of
your house, you are already being watched."
Sir Robert went on: "It may be you have heard that another
old man was murdered last night – his throat was slit, just
like your son in law."
"The murderer?"
"There are rumours about your daughter: some say she
wanted to run away with her lover. Others talk about a
soldier of the Duke of Norfolk, a certain James."
"James Wright. I met him at the court. And where did it
happen?"
"In a tavern in Eastcheap, the Boar's Head."
"Will you go there?"
Sir Robert nodded.
"And if I came with you? We would look less
conspicuous."
"Mmm… Yes, it could work. All right. Let's get going
before the curfew bells ring."
They took off their golden collars with their respective
guild emblems, and they each put on an old cloak, the one
light grey, the other dark. They crossed London Bridge,
mixing with the other people, and reached the tavern.

Above the door, the head of an enraged boar. Inside, on a
wooden table in dark letters:

Are you hungry? You may eat.
Are you thirsty? You may drink.
Are you cold? You can warm yourselves.
Here you will find food and drink,
bread, wine, fire and a good rest,
and a host of bottles and jugs.

They sat at a long table that smelled of beer. The air was thick with the smoke of cheap candles, a group of soldiers was sitting at a table at the other end.

They asked for beer. A young servant who looked rather too refined for such a place, brought them a jug. Sir Robert slipped her a coin: "For you. And tell us: do women come here?"

"Sometimes. Prostitutes, with the soldiers."

Sir Robert thought that Sarah could have found refuge there for some time. He asked: "Recently?"

"A few days ago."

When the inn-keeper appeared at the kitchen door, the young servant lifted the jug and pretended to be wiping the table with a cloth. "They took a room up above, I brought them food," she whispered.

"Did they often go out?"

"He did, a lot. She didn't. She called him James."

"And the woman, what was she called?"

"The woman? I don't know."

"Let's go and have a look above, they might have left some clues," murmured Sir Robert to Godfrey.

"May we have a look around?"

Another coin followed the first, "But make haste. The keeper…"

Helped by Godfrey, Sir Robert rummaged under the blankets, turned the mattress over, ran his fingertips through the dust on a shelf – but his expert eye did not find anything interesting. The room had a foul smell, two battered stools and a small table under a tiny window without shutters, the smelling blankets, the sticky floor.

When they were in the street again, Godfrey said: "Nothing at all. And that James, a ward of Norfolk, what do we know of him?"

"That he is in the North with Norfolk's soldiers. With that friend of his, that Barnaby Lowell."

"But James was in London on the day of the murder. You told me that he felt sick when he saw my son-in-law's body"

"That's true. And being a soldier, he must have seen many of them. Why did this one upset him so much?"

"And so?"

"So, we have to extend our investigations into the North."

'But how, but when?' he began to wonder.

"Tell me the truth: what happened?"

London, Whitehall

On Friday afternoon Sir Robert and his people had arranged to meet in their rooms at Whitehall in order to exchange news on the various investigations undertaken. But Sir Robert, who should have been the first to return, was late. When he finally arrived, his clothes, his hands and his face were covered in mud.

"Holy Virgin, what has happened to you?" had exclaimed Margery under her breath.

"Nothing, nothing. I just tripped and fell."

It took only a glance on Constance's part for her to see that he was lying – besides which he smelt strongly of beer: "Tell us the truth: what happened?"

And while Margery fetched a towel and poured some water from a pitcher into a basin, Sir Robert retreated to the end of the room to change his clothes. He then sat down, hesitated a moment, sighed, then finally accepted defeat:

"It was when I had finished at court and stopped briefly at the Old Mitre," he said.

"The tavern? And what were you doing there?"

"A beer, ears cocked, the odd question here and there."

Again he hesitated. "Well, perhaps I stayed rather too long. At a nearby table there were two rough-looking fellows. They were watching me. After the third beaker, when I made ready to leave, these two left with me. Once outside…"

He rose and went to wash his face and hands. The water was cool and refreshing, the precious soap given by Queen Kathryn to Lady Constance smelt of olive and laurel.

"Once outside, they followed me, then stood on either side in front of me. I asked: 'Who has sent you?'

And they: 'What would you pay us if we told you?'"

Sir Robert passed his fingers through his still-damp hair: "At that moment a patrol of the King's guards arrived and the two fled. Not before they had pushed me face down in the mud."

He ended: "But I'll return there, oh yes, I'll return there…"

Vanished into thin air

London, Whitehall

Late on that afternoon Sir Daniel, Sir Barnaby's friend, returned to Sir Robert's rooms in Whitehall together with the young Philip. Sir Daniel had a bandaged head and a swollen eye, Philip was limping badly. Sinking down onto a bench, his back against the wall, Sir Daniel began his account:

"I went round the ale-houses of Southwark. All the same: dingy, stinking of beer, at the tables groups of men gambling. They get drunk, argue. No result. So I go further towards Bishopsgate, up by Fish Street and Grace Church Street."

He thought for a moment: "Also the last tavern of the day, the Ship, if I remember correctly, was full of men drinking and going upstairs with prostitutes. I sought to catch some of the conversations while I was drinking my beer: very slowly, as I was already unsteady on my legs. The landlord watched me from the kitchen doorway. At a certain point he beckoned me.

'Good, this is it, I thought.'

He says to me: "You're not of this district, what are you doing here? You come to spy?"

So I told him that I have a sick mother, that I've found no-one in my village to treat her, that I'm looking for a woman who knows about medicine, and that, if knows someone, I can pay well."

He looks at me closely: "I'm telling you, I've seen you before, that's who you are, you were in the king's escort at Westminster and were wearing the livery of some lord. You're a proper spy."

And down came the ladle in a shower of blows on my head, I barely managed to escape."

"Who took care of you?" asked Sir Robert.

"Philip was in the neighbourhood, we had an appointment, we were to come back together. I was bleeding, he took me to a nearby inn."

He added, laughing heartily: "Not that he was in much better shape himself."

"It's true, Philip: what happened to you? Why are you limping?", Lady Constance wanted to know.

Philip blushed and gave a warning look to Sir Daniel – the two had become friends: "I don't think it's appropriate to talk about it."

"Not appropriate? But we want to know everything!" pressed Lady Constance.

"I, really..."

"Please, Philip, out with it," pressed Sir Robert, "otherwise we'll have Sir Daniel tell us what happened."

And he winked behind his spectacles.

Philip sighed: "Well, all right, this is how it went. I called in at all the inns in Southwark, but I had been seen with Sir Robert, they know about the inquest into the merchant's death, no-one would answer my questions. Whether they're Anglicans, papists or spies, people don't speak, they're afraid. I asked Daniel's advice and headed towards Bishopsgate. But even there they weren't forthcoming."

The young man's face went red: "I thought that in order to learn something I should flirt with the landlady in one of the inns."

He fell silent, he couldn't continue, he looked imploringly at Constance.

"Interesting," chuckled Sir Robert. "And she, the landlady?"

As Philip still didn't speak and grew even more scarlet, Sir Daniel intervened: "She took him seriously. He's a handsome young man, look at him. A poet, a dreamer, well-mannered. Clean and smart. She devoured him with her eyes, and took him to the room upstairs."

"Let us not go into details."

"And so I shall stick to the bare facts: sordid though they are. Well, before the inevitable could take place, her man returned home and kicked our friend up the backside and sent him flying down the stairs."

After they had finished roaring with laughter, Margery was holding her sides and Sir Robert was wiping his eyes – Lady Constance wished to make her own report: "We discovered nothing, nothing at all," she concluded. "She's disappeared into thin air and we have to be careful how we proceed."

"Vanished into thin air," confirmed Sir Barnaby who entered the room at that moment. There were dark circles around his eyes, his clothes were unkempt, his hair ruffled: "My friend Agnes gave me some addresses, I went round all the brothels in Southwark."

There was another flash of amusement in the eyes of those present, immediately quenched when he continued: "I spoke with the girls – they are good creatures, often they have a child to keep in some part of the realm. They didn't want money, they will tell me if they learn anything. But in any case the day of the trial draws near: what will happen if she does not appear?"

Sir Robert knew well what would happen and he felt a heaviness in his heart. He went to the window, opened it in order to breathe more freely: a red sunset illumined the river, a cold gust of wind invaded the room.

"If she doesn't appear she'll be condemned to the gallows. But in these past few days I've been asking myself what the warder's wife could have meant by the words 'Sarah knows a place to go, and nobody would think of looking for her there. They would take her in that place, because she knows how to care for certain kinds of people.'"

'Who might these people be,' wondered everyone.

'Who might these people be?'

London, Whitehall

Sir Robert repeated: "They would take her in that place, because she knows how to care for certain kinds of people.' And who would these people be?"

There was a rush of responses:

Philip: "Where nobody would think of looking for her – and thank heaven for that."

And Margery: "And who would be those 'certain kinds of people'?"

Lady Constance: "And since we have considered all the plausible hypotheses, don't you think it's now time to consider the implausible ones?"

Margery looked up from her sewing: "I should have told you something, but I was afraid to."

She hesitated: "You've always made fun of me for what you call my superstition, but at this point... Sir Robert, may I speak?"

"Don't be afraid."

"Well, Cecily learnt that Sarah had fled from prison. She realized that I was worried. She says that she knows a seer, one who has found missing people before. One such was at

the bottom of a well, in the river, under a heap of stones. "Why don't we go and see her, you and I?" she proposed."
There followed such a silence that Margery became fearful: "I beg your pardon, don't think badly of me."
Sir Robert went to sit beside her on the bench, put his arm around her shoulders: "No, come, speak your mind."
"Sir Robert, do you remember six years ago, when we came to London because you had to investigate the death of that fellow, the servant of Queen Anne Boleyn?"
"Master Crook, the man who spied on her for the king."
"Him. That woman foresaw a death by water for our beloved Alice. We didn't understand, and she drowned."

At those words Philip became pale, his expression one of shock, as if he had been struck suddenly in the back with a dagger. Sir Barnaby was about to ask him if he felt unwell, but Lady Constance whispered to him: "Not now, I'll explain to you later."
Sir Robert turned back to Margery: "Continue," he encouraged her.
"That old woman is still alive. She's called Nan Chetwood. She lives near the docks."
"And you wish to go there?"
"It might be useful."
"If the woman helped us to find Sarah. If she could reveal who hated the old man enough to kill him," said Sir Robert, giving voice to the anguish that tormented him by day and kept him awake at night. "Yes, Margery, it might work. We shall do so, if we're all agreed."
They were.
"I should like to come with you," said Sir Barnaby.
And Sir Robert: "Tomorrow is Saturday. The Court Chamberlain has invited us to a bull-baiting. We could go

together as far as London Bridge, then you three could go on to the docks."

"Heaven bless you," said Margery.

Bull baiting

London, Southwark

The day was fine, although cold again. As the company made their way towards London Bridge, Sir Robert asked Sir Daniel: "Do you know anything about Queen Kathryn? Norfolk has gone north and we have no-one else to give us news."

"At the moment she's being kept in the monastery of Syon Abbey, waiting for Parliament to pronounce judgement."

"Which means?"

"That it will decide what is to be the sentence, whether her conduct before marriage to the king was improper, or whether she cuckolded him afterwards. In the former case it will mean imprisonment for life, in the latter the scaffold."

"She's not yet twenty," lamented Lady Constance.

"That didn't prevent her from dallying with half of the court. Now it seems she's asked for a block the same size as that for the execution in order to practise dying. 'I don't wish to appear like a silly country girl,' she's been reported as saying."

"Poor creature," sighed Margery.

"Don't waste your pity," commented Sir Daniel.

When they had crossed London Bridge, Margery, Cecily and Sir Barnaby made their way towards the docks area, the others headed towards the bull-pit, where that day bull-baiting was taking place. "Gambling is a real passion for Londoners," explained Sir Daniel. "They bet on everything: cocks, dogs, bears, bulls, monkeys. You will enjoy yourselves."

"I doubt it," said Lady Constance.

The pit was a hexagonal structure, coloured white on the outside, containing banks of steps under cover around an open area in the middle. At that moment some bulls which had crossed the city decorated with flowers and ribbons were being pushed into a fenced area on the side. There was huge crowd, as many as a thousand people, of all ranks, men and women, ordinary folk, craftsmen, merchants, nobles – standing room cost a penny, to be seated on one of the benches in the gallery cost two-pence. At the centre of the pit there was a stake, to which the animal to be baited was attached by a rope about fifteen feet in length, long enough to allow it to move. There it would be attacked by the dogs. From the blood-stained sand on the ground arose a nauseating stench.

When the pit was full, four heavily-built men led in a large bull and tied it to the stake. In came two wretched-looking mastiffs which started to circle it. Sir Daniel explained: "These animals are trained to bite the bull's nose and not let go. The nose is a very sensitive part of the bull, and gripping it in this way has the effect of immobilizing it. Then the other dog goes for its throat. The dogs that are wounded or killed get replaced up to certain number, but the bull has to fight to the end."

The show began. The older mastiff kept low, so as to avoid the bull's horns. The younger one was less cautious, the bull caught him on his horns, span him round and tossed him in the air amidst the cries of the spectators, and when he landed back down, the bull raged over him and with horns and hooves reduced him to a bloody pulp. But whilst the bull had his head down, the other dog sank his teeth into his nose, and this paralyzed him. The crowd shouted and urged him on to fight, an attendant took away what was left of the first dog, and a white-faced Lady Constance asked her husband to take her out. "I don't feel very well," she said.

Sir Robert took hold of her by the waist, pulled down the hood of her cloak, and did likewise with his own.

"Why?" she asked.

"I've seen the King in the central gallery. Excited, purple-faced. With him Joseph Godfrey. The last thing I want at this moment is that he remembers me."

Sir Daniel stayed behind to enjoy the show, Philip kept him company.

"Beware of your friends."

London, Southwark

Meanwhile Cecily, Margery and Sir Barnaby had gone into the narrow dockland streets: noisy, reeking of horse droppings, urine and kitchen refuse. The houses were poor, of wattle and daub, many with thatched roofs – those most in danger of catching fire.

Cecily knew these places well, she had been born in the neighbourhood, her father had worked on the ships. She walked briskly, here calling out to a woman at a window, there exchanging greetings with a workman at the door of his workshop. In these workshops were being prepared rigging, ropes, sails, timbers, and there was a smell of resin and bitumen; further on, towards Billingsgate, could be found the warehouses and the mooring places for the ships. Halfway there, all of a sudden Margery gestured to Cecily to slow down. She was panting. All three seated themselves on a stone bench by a small dilapidated house, and Sir Barnaby took the opportunity to ask: "Why was it that yesterday, when the seer was mentioned, that Philip seemed to take ill?"

"It's a story that goes back six years," replied the woman. And she explained to him how at that time Philip had fallen in love with one of the Queen's maids of honour and how their love had ended in tragedy.

"The girl drowned in the river, as the seer had predicted. Was it an accident? Remorse on her part? We shall never know," said Margery.

"I still remember it, it was the talk of the city," added Cecily. "They found her downstream, in the Greenwich area, it was said, in a bend of the river where the current is less strong."

"And Philip," concluded Margery, "still feels the wound."

They proceeded on their way. Cecily knocked at a shabby door, painted blue, just under a tavern sign, a white swan on a green meadow. The door was opened by a cross-looking servant: "Don't you know that we're closed at this hour?"

When they asked after Nan Chetwood she pointed to a staircase which led to the floor above, and she left them in a half-lit, foul-smelling entrance-hall. They went up, holding on to the rickety banister with one hand, and feeling their way on the wall with the other. They saw two doors. They knocked. At the first no-one replied, at the second they heard something muttered. Sir Barnaby pushed it open and went in first.

An old withered woman, wrapped in several layers of wool which smelt mouldy, was sitting on a stool in front of a low bed, next to a burning brazier. On a table – the woman must have been awake a good part of the night – , a cheap candle clock had reached the final hour and gave out a flickering light and acrid fumes.

The old woman looked at Margery. "I recognize you," she said, and, unexpectedly, smiled, revealing some blackened teeth. "You are a good woman. You did all you could. If the one you tried to protect drowned, she went her way in peace."

She pointed at Cecily: "John's niece. May Heaven keep you."

She had them sit down on the bed.

The old faded eyes stared at Sir Barnaby: "I know why you are here."

She gestured to him to give her his hand, which she held between her own. "Your heart is full of darkness. Before there was hatred, now fear."

She turned his hand over so that the palms faced upwards. 'Whatever can she make out in this light?' wondered Margery.

The seer clasped his hands in hers, closed her eyes, breathed deeply, seemed almost to fall asleep. The others looked on in silence, Cecily had forewarned them. Eventually she gave a quiver. She said: "It's no longer a time of fear. Look for her, you will find her."

A pause. "Confusion. Chaos. She's carrying your daughter in her womb. A journey, you will go a long way away."

Sir Barnaby would have liked to know where this long way away was, and whether they would be left in peace. He asked "Tell me more."

"Plots. Betrayal. Blood. A woman on the scaffold. I see a head rolling in the straw. A castle. Low clouds, fog. Darkness. Soldiers' cries. Beware of friends, their weapons can kill."

"And...?"

Nan Chetwood seemed to come to herself, looked at him with feverish eyes: "Enough. Go away. Get out," she shouted, frightened, as if a ghost had passed by her.

They wanted to pay something, she shook her head. Sir Barnaby put a silver coin on the table, next to the candle.

When they went out onto the street, disconcerted by what they had heard, a gust of wind and a blast that smelled of river water welcomed them. They breathed with relief, as if freed from a nightmare. But a worrying question was insinuating itself into their thoughts: from whom, from which of their friends should they protect themselves?

Saint Mary of Bethlehem

London, Whitehall

Nearing London Bridge they met Lady Constance and Sir Robert, and Sir Barnaby repeated word for word their conversation with the old woman.

"You will find her, she said? We must give it some thought," said Sir Robert. "Let us dine together in my rooms."

Sir Daniel and Philip joined them when they were already at dinner. "You returned with the sovereign's escort?" asked Sir Robert.

"We came away a little before so as to avoid the crowd. Two bulls were killed and a dozen dogs. "And you, Barnaby, what did the seer reveal to you?"

Sir Barnaby reported: "She said that the time for fear had passed, that we must act. Search for Sarah, because she's expecting a son of mine."

"A daughter, a little girl," corrected Margery, contentedly.

"She said that I shall find Sarah, that we shall go away. Then she saw a head roll in the straw."

"Queen Kathryn," confirmed Sir Daniel.

"Confusion and disorder. And to beware of friends."

"Of friends?"

"'They have weapons which kill,' "she said. This I don't understand. You here are all my friends."

"There's no-one who envies you?" asked Lady Constance. "No-one you've wronged?"

"I have never wronged anyone. Except that..."

He looked around, dismayed. He stopped.

When the dinner was over a servant brought in some cream cakes and a fragrant Chablis from Burgundy. It was late when they parted, having arranged to meet the following morning to plan further enquiries.

So as not to attract attention to himself Sir Barnaby had not returned to court, but was lodging with Sir Daniel in an inn near the towers of Aldersgate. The two left together.

Later Lady Constance was brushing her hair at the dressing table and Sir Robert, already in his night-shirt and with a woollen nightcap on his head, was sitting on the edge of the bed, his feet in slippers dangling and a blank expression on his face.

"I have seen all sorts over the years. Crimes of hate, passion, madness. But I have never had a case like this," he said despondently. "Perhaps I have become too old to understand. I have got the confessed criminal, but I cannot have him arrested because basically he is not guilty. In fact, as the days have gone by, I have become fond of him so that I want to convince myself of his innocence."

He gave a cough and pulled the woollen shawl around his shoulders. "I must find someone who is accused of killing her husband, and if they find her before we do, they will hang her, but I am sure that she's innocent."

He went on: "I should denounce her father who says he caused his sister's death, but I will not do it because I am convinced that there was no intention to kill, and that it wouldn't be right deprive Sarah of her father, should she come back home."

He said nothing for a few moments. "About Sarah," he went on, "we have looked for her in churches, taverns, inns, hospitals: and found not a trace. And over everything looms the shadow of a sovereign who is anxious to put someone to death, whoever it is. If I do not solve the case soon, it will be my neck that feels it."

"He declared that he held you in great respect, but isn't it true that all your steps have been dogged by him and his men?" complained Lady Constance.

Sir Robert made to get into bed. "A place where no-one would imagine, where she could look after certain people. What the devil did she mean?" he muttered.

The light from candles and the fire cast long shadows on the walls. Suddenly, reflected in the mirror, Lady Constance saw her husband open wide his eyes and strike his forehead with his hand:

"Fool, stupid old fool!" she heard him exclaim.

"Holy Virgin, are you alright?"

"Bedlam, that's where she's fled to."

"Bedlam?"

"Bedlam, Bedlam – Saint Mary of Bethlehem, the hospital for the insane!"

Bedlam, hospital for the insane

London, Bishopsgate

As soon as it was light Sir Robert sent a servant to tell Sir Barnaby to come immediately to Whitehall. Then the two of them, once past St Paul's Cathedral, made their way across Cheapside and Bishopsgate Street towards St Mary's of Bethlehem, next to St Helen's Priory beyond the city walls. Their horses' shoes rang out on the cobblestones shiny with rain.

"Sir Robert, what made you think of Bedlam?"

"Do you remember the words of Margaret, the Clink governor's wife? 'Sarah knows somewhere to go and no-one would ever imagine that she was there. They would take her because she knows how to treat certain kinds of people.' And then those of the seer, 'noise, confusion'. Madness, perhaps? I eventually managed to connect these two things."

"If she should be there, how do we get her out?"

"We are not going to take her away. First let's find her, then we will decide. Lower the hood on your cloak so that we shall not be so easily recognized. Don't forget that the King's men too are looking for her?"

St Mary of Bethlehem, the hospital for the insane, was situated outside a gate at the north of the city, Bishopsgate, beside St Helen's Priory. It consisted of a courtyard in the middle of a few low buildings in grey stone, a garden, a church surrounded by a graveyard. Founded as a priory, with time it had become a hospital and finally a retreat for the insane. It was infamous both for the disorder that reigned there and for the terrible conditions in which the patients, numbering about thirty, were held. The violent ones were chained to the floor or the walls. Others were allowed out to beg for alms. Control was in the hands of overseers paid by the local parish or by relatives who wished to free themselves of an inconvenient member of the family. The cesspit was rarely cleaned, the kitchen stank of refuse, and the place was full of beetles, fleas and lice. The only relief came from a few widows who brought a little food and took it on themselves to care for the sick.

Sir Robert and Sir Barnaby pounded on the door with the huge lion-headed knocker.
"Someone who takes care of the sick? Young, brown-haired? Yes, she often used to come here."
Sir Barnaby felt faint. "Used to come, and now?"
"But you, who are you?"
"Her friends."
"You don't want to take her away?"
"So she's here."
The servant who had opened the door – a young lad with an artful manner, round faced, buck-toothed and with an unpleasant odour of sweat about him – , looked them up and down, realized that he could make something from these gentlemen and pretended to hesitate before a coin got him to talk: "She's in there," indicating a door at the end of the courtyard.

As they crossed the garden they saw an old man wrapped in a once-elegant black cloak. He was looking at the ground, walking round in circles and holding an excited debate with himself.

They entered a room which was lit by a small window barred with iron on the outside. It was cold, but the window panes were clean, the floor swept, a table and bench well-polished. Sarah was seated at the table next to a pale old man with a mild expression, who was wearing a worn-out tunic and whose eyes fill with tears while she put ointment on his forehead and smiled as she talked, as with a child. "Brother Oswyn, it's nothing. Doesn't it hurt less now?"

The two pulled back their hoods. When she saw their faces, the young woman froze, her expression showing in turn amazement, anxiety, relief. She got up, Barnaby went to meet her, and she rushed into his open arms.

Sir Robert would have liked to leave them alone, but what about the old man? So he went and sat down next to him. On the table was left some of Sarah's little store of medicines. He finished dabbing the wound then bandaged the head. The man kept repeating in a faltering voice 'The Lord be gracious to you, the Lord bless you."

Eventually Sir Robert held him under the arm and matching his to the other's small steps, helped him out. Again, wrapped up so as to avoid being recognized, he left him with the servant, who had remained at the door to eavesdrop.

"What's happening, sir?"

"Don't worry, everything's fine. Why don't you want Mistress Tiler to leave?"

"In the past she used to come every so often, just to treat the sick. But now she's always here, she takes care of everything." He adopted a virtuous tone. "It's me that helps her pull up pails of water from the well, to wash the floors, to clean the pots, to prepare the vegetables."

"Well done. Now take this man away."

Seeing him hesitate, he raised a finger to his lips: "Shh, go on. Later there will be money for you, if you know how to keep a secret."

He sat down on a stone seat, then got up because it was cold, and passed the time walking up and down the cloister, enfolded in his cloak with the hood pulled down.

"You have never looked so beautiful."

London, Bishopsgate

In the meantime Sarah and Barnaby were sitting on a bench under the window, close to each other. As the day gradually dawned the light revealed her face, still bathed with tears.

"When Matthew died, you disappeared. I feared that you had done something terrible."

"With all my heart I had wished him out of the way, but I did not intend, I swear to you, I had no desire that he should die."

"I searched for you, I didn't know where to find you, I was desperate," she interrupted him. "That morning, when they summoned me to the spot, I caught a glimpse of you from behind, on horseback: you were leaving."

"I was distraught. And later, how could I contact you without also compromising you? He was your spouse, I a stranger. Then the order to depart, suddenly, early in the morning, and we left London for Berwick by forced marches As soon as I learned of your arrest, I hurried here."

Looking in her eyes he noticed a different light there, a softness which was new to him. "Is it true that we are expecting a baby?"

She smiled at him.

"We'll call him Joseph, after your father," said Barnaby.

With the tips of her fingers she caressed his cheek: "We'll call her Leah, like your mother," she replied.

For a moment they laughed, then she became serious again, she glanced down at her hands ruined by work which she was not used to, sought to hide them under her apron. Barnaby took them between his own and raised them to his lips: "You have never looked so beautiful," he murmured.

She held him tightly again: "How were you able to find me?"

"We searched all over: taverns, inns, brothels. We drank barrels of beer, we became involved in all sorts of escapades, eventually Sir Robert had a sudden inspiration that you were here."

"His investigation into Matthew's death?"

He hesitated: "He knows nothing yet..."

By now the sun had fully risen, beams of yellow light streamed through the window. Sarah rose: "Sir Robert will be dying of cold there outside, I shall go and call him," and she headed to the door.

All three of them came to sit at the table.

"Sir Robert, thank you for coming to the Clink."

Sarah wrapped the thick woollen shawl which he had brought her more tightly around herself. "When the gaoler helped me escape that night, I wanted to let you know, but it was dangerous. Then here, there has been so much work. That old man, whom you have just finished treating..."

"He has the air of a man of God," observed Sir Robert.

"He was one. Brother Oswyn, who used to preach in the parish of St Etheldreda, near to Charterhouse Street. During one of the recent epidemics, of what they call the 'sweating sickness', he witnessed a lot of suffering and tried to do something to help, to bring comfort. He buried young and old, mothers and their babies. Many who were well in the morning dropped down dead in the evening."

Sarah looked at him steadily, her voice sad. "A woman of the parish lost her husband and two little ones in that way. One Sunday morning she showed up at the door of Brother Oswyn's monastery, dishevelled, skeleton-like, with a child in her arms, her last one, who was dying – its face stiff, its eyes huge. 'Help me!' she begged. He put his hands on both of them, blessed them, and went into the church because it was time for his sermon. He was exhausted, days and nights without rest – he fainted in front of the altar.

She sighed. "When he came to, he was groaning, tearing at his cassock, shouting out: 'And am I to preach about a God of grace? Of a Father omnipotent and merciful?' Since that day he has been here, he no longer remembers anything, though occasionally he makes the sign of the cross, as if in blessing."

They heard some shouting in the corridor and the two men just had time to get up and pull their hoods over their faces. The door opened and the hospital warden, a large, red-faced man, came in the room. "You, what are you doing here? What do you want from us?"

Sarah sensed the danger sign: Sir Robert's hesitation in replying clearly signalled 'Be careful not to leave any traces'.

"These gentlemen are personal friends of the sovereign," she said. 'They know me because my father is the King's physician."

Immediately the man became obsequious: "I'am honoured."

And Sir Robert: "It's time for us to go. Sarah, I am pleased to find you well and treated with respect." He turned to the warden: "We shall be back here very soon."

"So you won't take her away then?" said the man, anxiously twisting the large bunch of keys that hang from his belt.

And as Sir Barnaby was about to say something, Sir Robert took him by the arm and led him out.

"Why did you drag me away?" asked Sir Barnaby when they are outside.

"I didn't want that man to be able to come back on us. Sarah understood immediately and introduced us without giving away our names. And she herself won't say anything."

"Forgive me, I hadn't realized. My head's in a muddle. The happiness of finding her again, the thought of what the future holds."

They had to wait until they got back to Whitehall before continuing their conversation. As they left Bedlam and re-entered the city, they found the streets full of people and resounding to the cries of porters

and water-carriers, the din of carts and the neighing of horses, to the hammering of tin-platers and blacksmiths, carpenters and coopers. In all districts the shutters of the workshops had been drawn back: the cobblers of Cordwainer Street, the furriers of Welbrook, the stall-holders of West Cheap, the candle-makers of Lothbury, the jewellers of Old Jewry, the makers of religious images in Paternoster Row, the wine-merchants of Vintry. Smells, noises, voices, dealings: the city had woken up.

'But how do we get her away?' was what each of them was wondering now.

"It was last night."

London, Whitehall

At Whitehall, while waiting for Sir Robert and Sir Barnaby to return from Bedlam, Lady Constance, Margery and Sir Daniel wrapped in their cloaks had gone down into the gardens. Sir Daniel gave his arm to both ladies, and they by common instinct confided in him.

"It was yesterday evening," said Lady Constance. "All of a sudden he slaps his forehead, opens his eyes wide, I'm startled, I think he's been taken ill, he shouts: "Bedlam, that's where she's hidden herself!"

"The unlikeliest of places, among the demented. Yes, she must have chosen it for precisely that reason. Let us hope that we can find her again. On the journey to Scotland Barnaby and I rekindled our old friendship. He's still the fine lad he used to be, and he's madly in love with that Sarah. What's she like this woman?"

"Not very good-looking," muttered Margery. For her to have a child outside wedlock was always reprehensible. Even though there had been well-known examples: had not King Henry had two children by his mistress Mary Boleyn, sister of his second wife, Anne Boleyn? And Henry Fitzroy, from his mistress Bessie Blount?"

"Sarah is attractive, and has charm," said Lady Constance. Then, remembering the reproving look she had shot her husband before Sarah's interrogation, she wished to redeem herself: "And then, one who cares for the poor without asking anything in return *must* be a good person."

"What will happen now? Did Sir Robert say anything about the investigation?" Sir Daniel asked again.

"He has to answer for it to the sovereign. He's anxious, he broods, sleeps badly, torments himself – cannot separate himself of the thought of that dead man. And in any case the matter of the will is not settled, if the king's men find her, Sarah will go to prison and from there straight to the gallows at Tyburn.

When Sir Robert and Sir Barnaby passed through the gateway of Whitehall, the three went to meet them, keen to know: had they found her? Was she safe and sound? But there were other people around and the faces of the two gave nothing away. Sir Robert ordered: "Let us go to our rooms."

"Yes, she's at Bedlam," said Sir Robert. "She's well. Now Sir Barnaby will tell you everything, then we must decide what path to follow."

They drank some hot wine, slid the bolt on the door and, out of caution, withdrew to the furthest room. Lady Constance and Margery sat on the edge of the bed, Sir Daniel and Philip on the window-seat, Sir Robert took a stool, Sir Barnaby chose to remain standing, and paced backwards and forwards: "We found her, and in good health. She makes herself useful in exchange for board and lodging," he said, and recounted the episode with the friar.

"And she's expecting a child, isn't she?" Lady Constance asked him.

"I realized it from the way she looked at me. But she was extraordinarily calm. Then I understood what she was thinking: that if I should be accused of the crime – in truth I had every reason to remove the old man – , she would surrender in order to save me."

"And you, what do you think of doing?" asked Sir Robert.

"I shall not allow it. If they find her, I shall go to court and swear that I killed Matthew with these hands."

"A brilliant move. So your child will be raised fatherless because you will have been condemned for a crime you did not commit."

"I don't..."

But Sir Robert raised his hand and rose to his feet: "I beg your pardon, I must leave you. I have a meeting at Lincoln's Inn with Sir Geoffrey Clifford for a case that I was concerned with before all this pandemonium started. I shall return later. Come, Philip."

Lady Constance followed him into the other room: "Robert, do not fret, there will be a way out. You have said yourself many times that truth always prevails."

He collected his papers and placed them in Philip's leather wallet: "I used to think so, Connie, but now I'm no longer sure of anything. And when the king wishes to know, what shall I tell him?"

Flee: but where?

London, Whitehall

When Sir Robert had left, Lady Constance again bolted the door and came back into the room. "Sir Barnaby," she said, "have you anywhere safe you could escape with Sarah?"
He looked at her in astonishment: "Why?"
"It's simple. If you are not blamed, Sarah will go the scaffold. And if Sarah is not declared guilty and if the events surrounding Esther's death become known, it will be her father who goes to the gallows, and she will hate you all her life."
"She loves me."
"Today. And tomorrow?"
"We can flee."
"Good lad, now you see. That's why I asked you if you had anywhere safe to hide."
Sir Barnaby reflected for a few moments: "Certainly not in England, sooner or later we would be found. In Ireland, yes. My mother's family has links with the Fitzgeralds."
"The lords of Kildare?"
"Exactly. King Henry does not trouble about Ireland providing they pay their tributes. We could go north, to the Scottish border."

He grew excited as he spoke: "At Carlisle Castle there are fellows from my regiment, friends, who wish me well. They would welcome us. From there we could take a boat over."

"When you had arrived at the coast, I could secure you a passage on a ship," said Sir Daniel. "I know them all in that area."

"But Sarah will need money, warm clothes, medicines," observed Margery.

"She would find all that in the merchant's house. She could hide there while making preparations for the flight," suggested Sir Barnaby.

Lady Constance nodded to Margery. The two women went to the trunk which stood in the corner opposite the fireplace. They took out cloaks, dresses, tunics, they lifted the false bottom. Lady Constance drew out a small brown leather bag and handed it to Barnaby: "It is my money, I beg you to accept it."

Sir Barnaby made a show of pride, as if to refuse it, but then: "A loan," he said, "I shall pay it you back."

Margery whispered something in Lady Constance's ear and she withdrew another small bag, this time of canvas. Margery gave it to the young man: "It's not much, but with all my heart."

He embraced her.

Now it was Sir Daniel's turn to speak: "I shall provide for the costs of the journey north, we shall return together."

And Lady Constance: "I warn you: we shall have to inform Sir Robert of our plan, we cannot act without his knowledge. If he can, he will help us; if not, he'll pretend he knows nothing and we can proceed on our own account. But, please, say nothing about the money."

The company separated, they would meet again at dinner, on Sir Robert's return.

"C'est l'argent qui fait la guerre."

London, Whitehall

"So it's an escape you've planned behind my back," said Sir Robert that evening at dinner as he finished his wine. "No, I'm not annoyed Connie, but I seem to be the only one amongst us who is still using their head. And I'll explain why."

He began to count on his fingers: "One: you have decided that Sarah should escape from Bedlam, but have you devised how without raising suspicion? Because it must in no way lead back to us when she doesn't return there."

There was no reply. Sir Robert continued: "Two: Sarah hides in the merchant's house for a few days, but the building is now under the surveillance of the royal guard. Have you thought how to have her enter? And then how to have her leave?"

They looked at him in consternation.

"Three: Sarah flees with Barnaby – they will need money. Why are you blushing, young Barnaby? Money is important. Don't you know the old saying 'C'est l'argent qui fait la guerre'? Haven't you considered this point?"

Sir Daniel and the two women didn't blink. Sir Barnaby was the only one to go red – Sir Robert did not understand why.

"Four: we are at war with Scotland, wherever you go in the border region you'll need a safe conduct, and on this the name of the person to whom it is granted. Barnaby, he's going back to join his regiment, but Sarah, how can she obtain one?"

Sir Daniel: "I am on a mission for my lord of Carlisle and am returning to Cumberland from London, my safe-conduct is official, I even take precedence over all the couriers."

"We are talking about Sarah."

"Exactly: I'll say that she's my woman, that she's lost hers but that shall have another from my lord as soon as we arrive in the county. I am sure that my lord will grant her one without asking questions. I'll give her an Irish name, and you know how many in Ireland have dark hair and eyes after so many handsome Spanish sailors have been shipwrecked on the coasts there."

Sir Robert agreed: "It could work."

He reflected: "And after the king's men have searched all London, houses, churches, priories, cemeteries, hospices – which will take time – , and haven't found her, she'll be presumed dead. So the case will be closed. But, and this is another objection, she can never again return, she must sever her bonds, for ever."

It was clear that they had not thought of this either.

Sir Robert passed a hand through his hair: "To sum up: I received an official assignment from the king. When he summons me, I shall have to tell him that I have been unable to fulfil my charge, that I haven't discovered the killer, that as regards Sarah Godfrey I know that his men have been searching for her, as have we – his spies will have informed him of that – , that she seems to have vanished into thin air. I'll request that my responsibility be terminated. And may God protect me from the sovereign's wrath."

Sir Barnaby started to say something, but Sir Robert stopped him: "No. What's more, understand that of your plans I must know nothing. I must not and will not. Understand too that I shall instruct my people not to involve themselves further, and that you, Barnaby, are risking the gallows, and Sarah with you."

Rarely had Lady Constance seen him so bad-tempered. She took his hand: "Robert, we are all very tired. Let us go to bed, shall we?" He followed her.

After tossing and turning in bed for a long time, Sir Robert finally fell asleep, and, as sometimes happened, he dreamt he was invisible. He was in London, in the Court of Chancery, and he went to stand next to the clerks without being seen. He was able to read the most confidential documents, written on rolls of vellum: the sovereign's Orders in Council stamped with the Great Seal of England, statutes, rulings. Now, standing behind the King's representative – a bishop in gold-embroidered vestments, Sir Robert ran his eye over a decree which appointed him Chancellor of the Ecclesiastical Court, a prestigious office. He reflected that he would have to leave Cambridge and move to London. The bishop looked around, observed him, but his benevolent face changed into that of King Henry, disfigured by age. 'Sire,' implored Sir Robert, 'forgive me, I haven't been able to solve your case.' 'And I condemn you to the gallows,' barked the King.' He begged for mercy and the other shook him by the shoulders.

He woke up, his wife was rocking him to wake him from his nightmare.

Margery too had been dreaming: she was young, and on a clear April day her father was accompanying her to the altar of the small round church of the Holy Sepulchre in Cambridge. There were flowers everywhere from the gardens and the meadows around the city, and lots of friends. Under her cloak she had on a light-yellow satin dress which, as is the custom, she would wear afterwards on Sundays and feast days. He was wearing a shirt of Lincoln Green. In her dream she was trying to see his face, but she could not recall all the features. 'He's been dead a long time, my Thomas,' she thought. 'Many winters have passed since that day, but how is it that I don't remember what he looks like?'

Then she found herself in a cornfield, and where had the church gone? She was holding a baby in her arms, Benedict, her son: he smelt of milk. Together with her little one she saw herself reflected in a pool of water, and she was young and beautiful.

Sarah dreamt of Barnaby. They were in a white-washed thatched cottage near the sea, the sound of which she could hear on the rocks below. She was grinding herbs in a mortar; he, seated in front of the fire, was holding a baby in his arms. She could hear them laughing together. It was a touching sight, father and daughter together. Peace, at last. They were not expecting a visitor, but someone arrived at the door. She wanted to say something, a phrase reverberated in her head: 'Beware of your friends', that's what it was, but she could not find her voice and he did not respond to her gestures. She was woken by the cry of a sick old man in Bedlam.

The next morning the bells were ringing the Third Hour when Sir Daniel and Sir Barnaby knocked on the door of Sir Robert's rooms.

"To reach Whitehall," said Sir Daniel, "we have come on foot through various districts, we wished to learn if there was talk of Sarah. Nothing, though. However, there's turmoil in the city."

Sir Daniel explained: "The queen's relatives, all the Howards with the exception of Sir Thomas, have been tried for having concealed what they knew about Kathryn."

"Tried and...?" asked Sir Robert.

"Condemned to prison for life, and all their property — castles, lands, revenues, money — , confiscated to the Crown."

"And the Duke of Norfolk?" asked Lady Constance.

"Not he. From Scotland he wrote a letter to the sovereign protesting that he knew nothing of the queen's conduct, and laid the blame on his niece and on the elderly Agnes Howard, the Dowager Duchess of Norfolk, for not forestalling such wanton behaviour. They say that when the king's guards arrived at Lambeth Palace they found the poor woman , who is now over sixty, busy burning papers and trembling with fear."

"And Kathryn?"

"She'll be tried publicly, by Parliament."

'Will the king be there? And she, how will she seek to exonerate herself?' they all wondered.

Homecoming

London, Southwark, the merchant's house

When, in the afternoon, Sir Barnaby and Sir Daniel made their way to Bedlam, they found the city in gloomy mood and the people restless. Sir Barnaby knocked at the door of the hospital, Sir Daniel stayed back with the horses.

"I must speak with Sarah Godfrey, on an important matter," said Sir Daniel to the servant who came to open the door. The latter led them to a room where the inmates were sitting round a large table.

Sarah was beside a poor half-wit, a man of uncertain age but not old – she was feeding him and wiping the dribble from his mouth. A thick soup in wooden bowls gave out a rich smell of vegetables.

Sir Barnaby raised the edge of his hood and addressed a startled Sarah: "Sarah Godfrey, your friend Margaret is about to give birth, she is in much pain, she wants you near her. Bring your things and come with me."

And since she looked at him without comprehension, he added: "Be quick, I beg you, before curfew falls and it's no longer possible to go where you have to go."

Sarah understood the message, went briefly away to gather her belongings into a bag and followed him without a word.

When they were at the entrance Sir Barnaby said to the servant: "Tell the governor that Sarah Godfrey will be away for a few days, tell him that it was one of the king's gentlemen who came to fetch her, one whom he has already met."

"What name should I give, sir?"

"There's no need, he knows it."

They went out, the servant did not close the gate immediately and was able to see Sir Barnaby slip Sarah's knapsack into his own saddlebag and, having sprung on his horse, lifted the woman sideways onto the saddle in front of him.

The two left swiftly, followed by another horseman heavily muffled.

There was a guard outside Sarah's house in Southwark. As arranged with Sir Barnaby, Doctor Godfrey came out with two beakers of warm wine sweetened with honey and offered one to the man: "I observed you from the window. Have a drink with me, you must be frozen, here for hours."

"There'll be a change of guard soon, but thank you, I'll gladly take it."

Godfrey stood so that the guard turned his back to the house, so that the three friends could sidle in silently, from the courtyard at the back. When they had entered Godfrey seated himself on the doorstep and invited the other to do the same. They drank together, they spoke for a while: soon the good season, this year the river hadn't frozen, it might snow again, the worst of the winter was over.

Eventually Godfrey took the two empty beakers and went inside.

"Good night, Sarah."

London, Southwark, the merchant's house

That evening in the little ground-floor kitchen Godfrey, Sarah, Sir Barnaby and Sir Daniel conversed for many hours, in hushed tones, by fire-light only, the shutters closed, the curtains drawn, so that from outside not even shadows could be seen. They had some hot soup, then went upstairs where Godfrey, in order to catch the guard's notice, went to the window and extinguished the candle at the usual hour. Then all four of them withdrew into the room which had been the merchant's and which looked over the courtyard, their sole light that of the brazier.

Sarah clung to Barnaby, he kept his arm around her shoulders. He said: "Soon I must leave, there is much to prepare for tomorrow night. I am taking her away, Doctor Godfrey, but be assured that I shall love her for ever."

That morning the two men had opened their hearts to each other at length, without reserve. Witnessing the tenderness of the young man towards his daughter the old doctor had recalled his own love for her mother: with sadness, now, not bitterness towards providence. 'The Lord had given and the Lord has taken away,' he had finally accepted. 'May his will be done.'

And that evening Sarah had observed her father: shrunken, wrinkled with age, a tremulous note in his voice. 'It is as if I had not seen him for years, although until a few days ago we were here together, in the same house,' she had reflected.

Sir Daniel said: "Be careful: no-one must suspect that she is here. No friend, no neighbour. Keep her upstairs, only a chink of light from half-closed shutters. If anyone comes, have her lie on the bed: she can sleep, rest, the journey north that we are undertaking will be tiring."

"There's always someone in guard outside the house. How will you mange to lead her away from here?" asked Godfrey.

Sir Daniel explained it to him.

As they left the merchant's house, Sir Barnaby and Sir Daniel showed their safe-conducts as king's gentlemen to the guard, who was duly impressed. "Tomorrow evening we shall be here again, we shall come with a cart," announced Sir Daniel. "Doctor Godfrey will present us with a case of medicines that he preparing for the sovereign. Will it be you here?"

The man had a strong Welsh accent: "Unfortunately so, although I'd prefer the warmth of a tavern," he replied.

"So we shall see each other again," and the two departed into the night.

Left alone with her father, Sarah sat down on the bed which had been hers and her husband's and adjusted the pillows at her back.

"Father, I would like to go once more to the graveyard where Matthew is buried."

"You can see his grave from this window, you shouldn't go out, and from now on take care not to be seen."

The man put fresh coal on the brazier to revive it. He took a stool and sat down next to the bed.

"Sarah, I must ask your forgiveness."

She was unsettled by this, it was the first time that he had shown any affection when he spoke to her. A total lack of interest when she was young, that yes, and an overbearing authority when he had forced her to marry the old Matthew.

Sarah did not reply.

"When your mother died, my heart dried up," continued the man, without taking account of her silent hostility. "I let it turn to stone. I didn't want to feel anything for anyone, and when you came to me holding out your little hand and with a child's smiling face, I pretended not to notice you: my wound was still bleeding too heavily. 'I must not love any more, no more of this hell if fate robs me of her too,' I thought. And I made a show of not caring about you."

Now the man was speaking as if to himself. "Only when you disappeared, when I was left here alone, in the evening, at night, did I understand how much you were a part of me. I was frightened for you: they might have kidnapped you, raped you, thrown you in the river. Only then did I realize how much wrong I had done you. For all this I ask your forgiveness."

Perhaps Godfrey expected a reply, which was not forthcoming. So he continued: "This morning Barnaby spoke to me. He is young, but he knows what he wants. And he loves you. You will be happy with him, wherever you go. My sole regret is that I shall not see any more of you, now that…"

That moment of tenderness filled his eyes with tears. He broke off.

'Now that he knows how to love again,' thought Sarah, and in the dark she saw him for what he was: a tired old man who had loved her mother, and who would die alone. "Father, come with us," she said on an impulse.

Godfrey shook his head. "No, I must stay here, to cover your escape, to pretend to know nothing. You will be Sir Daniel's servant until you reach Ireland, he has explained to me, so no-one will be suspicious of you. Later on you will send me word when I become a grandfather."

Sarah closed here eyes: the sadness for past times, the regret, the wasted love: it was all too much for her. Her father thought that she had fallen asleep. He took a fur blanket from the chest and spread it over her.

When he was at the doorway he turned round to look at her: "Good night, Sarah," he said quietly.

Flee: but how?

London, Whitehall

The morning after Sir Daniel, who at that time was acting as Commissioner for Supplies for the county of Cumberland, explained to Sir Barnaby how his escape would be managed: "We shall get a covered wagon, we will buy food, cooking pots, blankets, two braziers, coal, firewood for when we camp."

"And the change of horses?"

"At the inns."

"We can't stop overnight in these places, the King's spies might spot Sarah."

"At night we shall stay near the soldiers' camps, that way we'll be protected from outlaws. I'm in Norfolk's army, I can make myself known to them. During the day, when we are going through villages, she must stay in the wagon, so no-one will see her. If they are questioned, the villagers will report having seen one of the many royal transports heading towards Scotland with supplies."

While Sir Daniel busied himself with the purchase, in the courtyard of the inn where they were staying Sir Barnaby checked that the goods delivered were properly loaded on the wagon. The wagon, which would be pulled by two strong horses, had solid wheels and five high wooden hoops, which would support the cover of thick white waxed canvas.

Later Sir Daniel came to relieve him, and Sir Barnaby made his way to Whitehall to Sir Robert Kytchyn's rooms, going over in his mind the confession that he would finally have to make.

"Who is guilty?"

London, Whitehall

During the time that these preparations were being made, Sir Robert was summoned urgently by the King. He found him seated in the Privy Council chamber, together with Archbishop Cranmer and some Members of Parliament. Seated in a huge chair, he looked enormous: bad-tempered with everyone, the small mouth and ironic eyes hemmed in by the layers of fat which weighed down his face. Sir Robert seemed to read hatred in his expression.

"Here is our coroner! What good news do you bring us?" he gurgled.

"Sire..."

"Tell me: how long is it since Matthew Tiler's death? Have you understood anything? What conclusions have you reached?"

'Three weeks have passed,' thought Sir Robert, 'and this is the final stage, the settling of accounts, the moment in which the axe is lifted up before it falls on the neck of the condemned man.' He recalled the words of Scripture: 'Be as cunning as serpents and as innocent as doves.'

Looking at the King he said: "I have worked night and day on this case, as no doubt you will have been told. I have questioned those directly involved in the affair and in turn those more remotely connected. I and my people have checked their times and movements. I have walked the dirty alleys of Southwark, drunk beer with felons, courted inn-keepers' wives, been punched in the face and been kicked in the kidneys. The results have always been the same: no one is guilty."

He cleared his throat, then he went on:: the conclusions have always been the same, no-one is guilty."
He added: "And do you know why?"
'Why?' wondered everyone in the room, which had gone suddenly quiet.
Sir Robert deliberately waited a few moments before replying. Then: "Simple: because Matthew Tiler was not killed."
"Ah no?" quizzed Henry ironically.
"No, Sire. When I examined the body, I wondered whether he might have died from heart failure. In the post-mortem the nature of the bruising and the hypostatic marks suggested this. But with the wound to the throat, I could not be sure and continued investigating." 'And if now he wants to know about the blood-stained dagger, what should I tell him?' he immediately thought.

But the King did not ask anything, he grasped a handful of marzipan sweets from a silver bowl on the table in front of him, and stuffed them in his mouth. "So he wasn't killed," he mumbled. "And what can
you tell me about that witch of a wife of his, who falsified his will and disappeared from prison?"
"I have her sought everywhere – prisons, churches, priories, inns, taverns, brothels, the criminal districts. I know that

your guards have done the same. Probably raped and killed in the Clink, her body in the river, likely carried out to sea."

The King rested his elbows on the arms of the bench and leaned forward towards Sir Robert, a spiteful look in his eyes: "I know that you have searched for her; however, rumours have reached me from Clink Prison that you don't believe that she is guilty. How can you think the opposite of what I do? Perhaps you would like to help her escape my justice?"

Sir Robert raised his arms in a gesture of submission, as if the idea horrified him.

"Beware," barked the King, pointing at him, "beware. If you were involved in some way in her disappearance, well then, my friend, you would regret being alive."

"Where have you taken her?"

London, Whitehall

Sir Robert emerged shaken from his meeting with the King, his legs trembling, his heart pounding as if it would burst. He felt drained, old and useless. In former times he would go into a church, sit down on a bench in the shadows, would think over that conversation. Perhaps he would make confession. But now, he thought, after the havoc that Cromwell had wrought with the churches...

So he left Whitehall, walked a little way along the riverbank and paused to watch the water flowing, his elbows resting on the low wall.

Certainly the King's threat could not be clearer. However, Sarah was not guilty. Can one send an innocent to the gallows just because of a tyrant's obsession? And the ferocity of that look, those words, 'you would regret being alive'. Demented, that's what Henry has become. And he, who had got Constance involved too. What horror awaited them both?

Having returned to his rooms at the palace, his gaze on the ground, his cheeks suddenly drooping, all traces of optimism gone from his eyes, he sat down by the hearth, his hands, which he held out to warm by the fire, still trembling. When from time to time his wife shot a glance in his direction, he pretended not to notice.

Sitting at the table, Philip worked on some papers, and Margery and Lady Constance seated opposite each other by the bay window were unravelling small skeins of coloured cotton. The afternoon light shone on the latter's red hair, and her tranquil beauty made his thoughts even more painful.

Resentful that Barnaby had dragged him into this affair, he did not move when the young man entered the room and the others approached him to ask for news. He recounted to them the departure from Bedlam: "I told her that her friend Margaret was about to give birth and that I had to fetch Sarah for her. She stared at me wide-eyed: 'I don't know any Margaret,' I thought she was going to say."

"Where was Sarah at that moment?" asked Lady Constance.

"In the refectory. When she understood, we left in a hurry. Sir Daniel was waiting for us with the horses."

"Might someone have recognized you?"

"Out of the question, we had our hoods well down all the time. The servant was the same as on the previous occasion, the one with the rabbit teeth. I told him that Sarah would be back in a few days, so they won't look for her at once."

"Where did you take her?"

"To her father's in Southwark."

"And to get in the house?"

"Godfrey had organized a diversion for the guard, with warm wine, we had planned it together. In the merchant's house we talked most of the night. Of the past, of the future, she close by me – she is grateful for your concern, Sir Robert – , and Sir Daniel, who replied to her father's questions.

"How did Godfrey behave?" Lady Constance asked.

"He has lived through weeks of nightmare: the murder of his son-in-law, the death of his sister, Sarah's disappearance. He has the look of someone who eats badly and sleeps worse, hollow cheeks, a shrivelled face. But when his eyes rested on his daughter, they shone. And as we were going upstairs to continue our conversation, I noticed that he held her hand like a child, so that she wouldn't stumble.

"I beseech you, listen to me!"

London, Whitehall

Now, his account over, Sir Barnaby sat silent, in his mind the echo of Sir Robert's words from some days before: 'From now on, understand that I wish to know nothing of your plans, that I shall order my people to have nothing to do with them; that you, Barnaby, are risking your neck, and Sarah with you.'

And what can Lady Constance have said to her husband to soften his attitude? Or the elderly Margery, who that day had murmured: 'Sir Robert, they are just two children, and life is so short...'

"Sir Robert," murmured Sir Barnaby eventually, "I know that you don't want to get involved in my doings." He clasped his hands together, as if in prayer: "But I beg you, listen to me."

And while the others hung on his words with bated breath, he made his confession: he told of how he had followed the old man on that freezing night in order to confront him, to finally settle accounts with him. Of how he had in mind to insult him, to pour out on him his bitter feelings, to shout in his face that he was a useless old man, who should step aside, get out of the way for good...

"But when I called to him by name he turned round," he said. "He put down the lantern, came up to me and put a hand on my shoulder: in the dark I thought he was about to pull out a dagger, so I pulled my own from my belt, and put it to his throat. He was shorter than me, and frail. He... he said: 'What do you want, my friend?'"

"And you?" asked Sir Robert.

"I was completely taken aback. Don't you realize? The man that I detested, who perhaps knew about his wife and me, called me his friend! Then, instead of challenging me, he suddenly started gasping, as if he couldn't breathe. He fetched his hand up to his chest, staggered forward, and fell against me..."

Sir Robert would have liked to ask him some questions, but Sir Barnaby was now desperate to unburden himself of the anguish which had consumed him day and night. He recounted how the other man had collapsed on the ground before he himself had been able to say anything. He spoke of finding his hands covered in blood, of his terror – the flight to the prostitute's house, the money and chain thrown in the river. The torment, the remorse. Then the sudden departure with the army for Scotland, and there the agony, the infinite pain of not knowing anything, of not having, or being able to get, news from London.

While Sir Barnaby stayed sitting by the fire, his shoulders hunched, his expression vacant, Sir Robert began pacing around the room. 'This explains everything,' he thought, 'Sarah pretending not to recognize Barnaby's dagger, searching for him at her husband's funeral – which he did not attend –, not wanting to say anything in prison. She is even prepared to let herself go to the gallows in order to protect him. And Barnaby, who in turn wants to save her and is ready to take the blame in order to prevent her being condemned in his place'.

He asked: "Why didn't you pick up the dagger?"

"But don't you understand? It is one thing to hate someone; it is another to find his blood all over your hands. I was terrified, I just ran away. Sarah is not involved. I am the guilty one. It is I who deserve to hang for this."

"Have you confessed all this to Sarah?"

"Last night, at her father's house. I told her everything: that I had provoked Matthew, that he had turned towards me, had drawn close and then had fallen on top of me. I had held him up. He had died in my arms."

"And Sarah?"

She only said: 'He was good to me. Tell me that he didn't suffer.' She understood. She forgave."

"And why didn't you tell me all this when you came back from Scotland?"

"Do you think that it would have been easy? I couldn't bring myself to do it. I…"

"Farewell, young Barnaby."

London, Whitehall

Sir Robert was aware of this. He stood in front of the young man: "Now listen to me," he said. "Let us be clear about this once and for all. You, Barnaby, were desperate to rid yourself of a weak and innocent man — an action unworthy on your part. But now that I have got to know you, I am convinced that you are not really to blame. That when you put the dagger to his throat, if you had seen the great frailty of the old man, you would have felt pity for him."

"If I only could go back!"

"But you cannot."

"Part of me would like to die."

"And Sarah, what would become of her?"

"Certainly," continued Sir Robert, "you had the motive, the means and the opportunity to get rid of the old man. A well devised murder. But you didn't do it. And yet, isn't the intention to do wrong already in itself a crime? Does it not deserve punishment? At this point, why should I of all people agree to your escape?"

"But if they don't escape," Lady Constance declared heatedly, "one of the two will be hanged. And so, what is the right decision when there is no certainty, or if the only certain thing is sending an innocent to the scaffold?

She paused. Then: "Why should it be you to deprive these two young people of their futures? To have children and children's children in which they can continue to live. To grow old beside one another, to become tender and considerate. Tell me: where is the dividing line between justice and revenge?"

Sir Robert looked directly at Sir Barnaby – there was a tenderness in his eyes. 'He could be my son,' he thought to himself, once again. 'And he didn't mean to kill. It was the dagger which pierced the merchant's throat, not him. It's true, how can I let him be hanged? Or Sarah, in his place? No, if I need to pretend, I'll do it. If I have to lie, I shall lie. And may God forgive me.'

He said: "Barnaby: if your knife thrust had killed him, it would have been evident in the post-mortem."

The other did not react, perhaps he had not understood.

Sir Robert continued: "So listen to me. From the clinical symptoms that the corpse presented – the amount of blood which flowed from the wound, the *livor mortis*, the significant congestion which had occurred on the neck and shoulders due to heart failure, I am convinced that the man was already dead when your dagger pierced his throat."

He got up, grabbed the young man by the shoulders, shook him: "But it is not now a matter of whether you are to blame for his death or whether the merchant passed away because the Good Lord chose to call him that night."

He passed a hand through his hair which, in recent days, had seemed to go greyer. He looked at Sir Barnaby, and at the others one by one. His face displayed various emotions: sadness, fear, but overall a new determination. 'After this, nothing is as it was before,' he thought. 'I myself am no longer what I was...'

There followed a long silence, in which everyone was immersed in their own thoughts. Even the fire in the fireplace appeared to have grown quieter, as if waiting to hear something important.

Finally Margery asked: "Couldn't Sarah make a plea for mercy?"

"But the outcome would be uncertain," replied Sir Robert.

"Robert," suggested Lady Constance, placing a hand on his arm: "if the plea was accompanied by a large gift to the Crown?"

He shook his head: "Worse still, because it would be like admitting guilt, and if the pardon was denied, the punishment would be inevitable."

"And so?" asked Sir Barnaby.

Sir Robert realized that the young man, and perhaps also the others, had not yet grasped the nature of his ordeal. They did not appreciate the anxiety, the responsibility, the burden of his choices. Enter into the anguish, the torment in his heart of having to decide about the future without knowing the consequences. To wash one's hands of the affair, like Pilate, or perhaps to betray, like Judas. But if the sovereign were to find out the truth, his own life and that of his household would be in danger. He saw in his mind's eye Constance climbing the ancient steps of the Tower, shivering in the filth, a prisoner in a dungeon. Dying of hunger, slowly. And all because of him.

He turned to Sir Barnaby and told him of his meeting with the King: "And so, you ask of me. Now listen carefully, because this is my decision, and Heaven knows it has been a harrowing one to make. Barnaby, forget about me, continue to live without us. We have been your friends, we have suffered with you, we have tried to cheat time by exploring all possible avenues. But now it's over, we can't go on with you any further."

"Which means?" asked Sir Barnaby.

Sir Robert reacted almost angrily: "Which means that you must get out of our lives. Do you follow me? That you will not tell us what you intend to do, where you plan to go, or with whom. We no longer wish to know anything about anything."

"Not even..."

"Not even. If we know nothing, we shall not be able to give you away, and can rest in peace."

He got up, went into the other room. They all thought that he would not come back, that it was a farewell. But they heard him searching around in a chest and saw him reappear with a heavy money bag in his hand. They watched startled as he handed it to the young man: "This will be useful."

"Sir..."

"Farewell, young Barnaby, farewell."

Flight to the North

London, Southwark

It was already dusk when a covered wagon, pulled by two strong Breton horses, halted outside the merchant's house, screening the entrance. Sir Daniel took the driver's seat, while Sir Barnaby followed with two other horses.

The lane was silent, the house in darkness, no light above the doorway, no noise from within. Behind the shutters, Sarah was ready with two bags of her belongings. The soldier on watch was sitting on the steps of the house opposite: he stood up and lifted his lantern to light up Sir Daniel's face.

Sir Daniel greeted him: "Ah, you are not my Welsh friend."

"No, Sir. Dafydd's not here: his wife's giving birth."

"Congratulations to him then! Dafydd knew that we would be coming to Doctor Godfrey's house to collect some medicine chests for the King."

He gestured towards Sir Barnaby, who was just that moment dismounting: "Come on, they must be already packed, hurry up and load them on."

And turning to the guard: "Do you have to stay here till dawn? It's a bitterly cold wind that's blowing."

He jumped down from the seat, wrapped his cloak round him and in his turn sat down on the steps in such a way that the soldier standing in front of him had his back to the cart.

"Cold it is. Lucky Dafydd, who's at home in the warmth."

"Not really. For anyone who loves their wife, it is a terrible time when she is giving birth. Have you a wife?"

"She's in Wales. Who knows when I'll see her again."

"You are fortunate that you haven't been sent to the North."

He got up, turned towards Sir Barnaby, who was remounting his horse: "Have you loaded up? Right, we can go. A good watch, my friend."

"Good night to you, sirs."

The man turned to sit down on the steps while the sound of the wagon gradually grew fainter and, as it turned the corner of Winchester House, the little company disappeared into the night.

When they had crossed London Bridge and arrived by the shortest route – Candlewick Street, Wallbrook Street and Cheapside – , at Aldersgate, Sir Daniel and Sir Barnaby showed their passes.

"Ah, King's officers. What are you carrying?"

"Supplies for our soldiers in the North. Do you want to check?"

The soldier waved them on.

They proceeded slowly northwards for a few miles, lit by the lantern which swung to and fro on its fastening below the cart alongside the metal pail which jangled with every bump, and soon they stopped near an encampment of soldiers in order to pass the night. Sir Barnaby made himself known, then returned to their small camp. Sir Daniel had lit a fire, on which a pot was boiling. Sir

Barnaby climbed up on the wagon. "It's all right, you can come out."

Sarah emerged sleepy from under the blankets, helped by Sir Barnaby, while Sir Daniel banged a spoon against the cauldron and shouted to them: "Enough of the softness, the soup is getting cold."

The three young people's meal was a cheerful affair, full of memories of the recent past: as for plans, Barnaby and Sarah did not dare make any yet. She was dressed like a boy, her hair pushed under a woollen beret and a hood ready to be pulled down: they had decided on this in case she should be seen by anyone.

While Sir Daniel finished cooking meat on a spit, oiling it with a stick and turning it continuously, Sir Barnaby opened the packet that Margery had given him for Sarah: "She went into her friend Cecily's kitchen and made these sweetmeats for you."

"Marzipan, ginger bread, biscuits. Good old Margery! When Sir Robert was questioning me, the room suddenly started to spin round: Lady Constance recognized my condition and hurried to help me. I would so much like to able to thank her."

And Sir Daniel: "I'll do it for you myself, I will be passing through Cambridge on one of my missions: but not soon, things need to quieten down first."

When it was fully dark, they draped blankets over the horses' backs, put out the fire, Sir Daniel wrapped himself in his cloak and beside a well-lit brazier settled down to take first watch. Sarah and Barnaby went inside the cart.

It was soon morning. They breakfasted on salted bacon, soft cheese and small beer, while the horses chewed their fodder from sacks hung round their necks. They gathered the remains of the unburnt wood, collected the braziers, set off, Sarah hidden inside the wagon, Sir Daniel and Sir Barnaby together on the driving seat, the other two horses which were following, tied behind the cart.

The days passed and they often overtook columns of soldiers that were marching towards Scotland to the sound of the drum: banners in the green and white of the Tudors, the standards of the King's knights, dust and commotion. Then peaceful villages, the small cottages with thatched roofs, the taverns where Sir Daniel stopped to buy food.
They crossed different counties with their market towns: Staffordshire, Cheshire with its rich soil, Lancashire overlooking the wide Irish Sea, the lovely quiet valleys of Westmorland.
Away from the villages, Sarah got down from the wagon to walk. Although cold, the days were not always wet; from time to time the sun came out from behind the clouds to send a sudden flush of colour across the trees and meadows. Despite some morning sickness, Sarah was well, her figure filling out, her eyes radiant.

One afternoon they stopped in the vicinity of an old convent, abandoned since the devastation wrought by Cromwell's soldiers. Some of the perimeter walls remained intact, a chimney black with soot could be seen in the roofless refectory, and the remains of steps which led nowhere.
Sarah cleared the damp leaves off a stone bench and sat down, Sir Barnaby and Sir Daniel wandered into the small graveyard which surrounded the building. The sun made the grey stones gleam amidst the tall grass. They read: 'Sister Jane Selwyn, 1510-1536', 'Sister Ursula Gardiner, 1512-1537', 'Sister Charity Gibbs, 1512-1537'.

"The nuns' burial ground," declared Sir Daniel. "When these women were born King Henry was married to good Queen Katharine, the princess of Aragon. England was a happy realm."

"That's what my mother told me. Then from France arrived Anne Boleyn, that beauty with dark eyes who bewitched the sovereign."

"And those were years of devastation. Who knows how these poor women died?"

A few nights later a messenger overtook them riding towards Berwick Castle with dispatches for the garrison there. Kathryn Howard had been confined to the Tower, and if the king did not pardon her, she would be executed within a few days. Her uncle, the Duke of Norfolk, had orders to return from Scotland to London immediately. On their arrival, there was just time enough for Sarah and Barnaby to retreat into the cart.

Journey's end

Carlisle Castle

At that moment Sir Daniel was warming some wine sweetened with honey, and offered some to the messenger and his men, who squatted with him around the fire. On their arrival, Sarah and Barnaby had managed in time to hide in the cart.

"Other news from London?"

"Did you hear about the merchant killed by his wife?" replied the messenger.

"We were still there when it happened."

"Now another merchant has been murdered, his throat slit, like with that other!"

"Have they found the killer?"

"There's someone, a certain doctor... bah, I don't remember the name... who's investigating it. So this one goes to the merchants' guild..."

Despite the cold of the night, Sir Daniel started to sweat heavily. He rose to his feet, pretended to be calm, refilled the men's beakers. Then he went to the cart and tied the covers together, in front and behind, in case one of the soldiers should wish to pry inside, or Sarah and Barnaby think to come out.

He returned to the fire. "He goes to the guild, and..."

"They tell him that there's a fellow that owes the merchant money. That perhaps he comes to plead with old Tiler, as the Southwark merchant's called, to tell him that he can't pay. The merchant threatens him, the other knives him."

"The man, who is he?"

"A poor fellow. A drunkard from the ale-house. He's mute, he speaks with his hands. His wife is a laundress but she's ill, one of their children dies of that malady that that makes you spit blood."

'No-one is spared,' thought Sir Daniel.

And the soldier: "When they shut him in Newgate Prison he makes wild gestures, he howls. He beats his head against the wall until it splits. And he dies."

"What about the wife and children?"

"There's a certain fellow, he's called Godfrey, who doctors the king. That coroner who doesn't understand anything, meets him at court, tells him about the poor wretch..."

Again Sir Daniel shivered: how was Godfrey involved now? What might he have said or done?

The reply came immediately: "That Godfrey tells him that in his son-in-law's bedroom, the merchant, old Tiler, the one who lent the poor man the money, he's found a note..."

"And what does it say?"

"That he pardons him the debt."

Standing up in order to continue his journey, the messenger concluded: "It seems instead that old Tiler's murderer was really his wife. It appears that someone has helped her flee. Patrols are looking for her all over the country..."

When the men had gone, Sir Barnaby and Sarah emerged from the cart. The three looked at each other in consternation: 'they are looking for them all over the country...'. With growing unease they wondered where, how, when they might have left traces. But there was no time to lose, they decided to leave immediately.

The journey continued for several more days and it was morning, even before the First Hour, when they finally came within sight of the city of Carlisle.

Like Berwick, Carlisle was a frontier city on the border of England and Scotland – founded by the Normans, occupied by the Scots, over the years this stronghold had been frequently besieged, lost, retaken by both parties. Now, in the reign of Henry VIII, the castle which dominated the city was furnished with a strong English garrison.

"I must leave you here," had announced Sir Daniel. "Barnaby, you see that wood a little way ahead, near the river, underneath the castle mound? Take shelter amongst the trees while I go and get a pass for Sarah. It will take some time. But be careful: under no circumstances should you approach the city walls: the king's soldiers are there, she would be in danger. Don't leave the wood, wait until I return."

In London, in the meantime, the young life of Queen Kathryn Howard had come to an end. As the chronicles would later relate, 'the Duke of Suffolk informed Kathryn that she was to die. From Syon House he and his soldiers led her to the boat that would take her to the Tower. She started to scream, they were obliged to bind her hands and feet and carry her bodily to the landing-stage. They rowed downstream to London Bridge, where she had to suffer the dreadful spectacle of the impaled heads of her lovers, Dereham and Culpepper. They had been there two months, had putrefied, and the smell and the sight were revolting. When they arrived at the Tower she was shut in the rooms where her cousin Anne Boleyn had been imprisoned: cold and damp. Suffolk had them give her more blankets.'

The chronicle continued: 'The execution took place in the early morning. She was terrified: they had to support her as she climbed the steps of the scaffold. A young woman, alone: there was no-one who cared about her.

That morning, dressed in black, all the members of the King's Privy Council, except Norfolk, were present in the Tower courtyard. It was raining, the platform was spread with straw. She asked for forgiveness for her own faults, exhorted obedience to the sovereign. They tucked her hair in a white bonnet so that it wouldn't hinder the headsman's task, bound her eyes, made her kneel down in front of the block. She started to cry out 'I don't want to die!'

When the axe fell on her snow-white neck, the blood spurted out over all the dignitaries assembled under the scaffold, and the head rolled away. The executioner knelt down to search for it in the straw, picked it up by the hair and lifted it aloft, as custom demanded, then placed it next to the block. Two servants draped a black sheet over the still-kneeling figure, as no coffin had been prepared. Eventually the head and body were taken to the royal chapel of St Peter-within-the-Tower, where her cousin Anne Boleyn was buried.'

"Alone and free. And happy."

In the woods near Carlisle

While these events were taking place in London, in Carlisle, Sir Barnaby and Sarah were sheltering in the woods near the river. A veil of mist was rising from the fields, the fortress in pink stone, squat, menacing, dominated the hilltop. The smell of moss and damp earth, birds among the branches: intense, unexpected peace.

Barnaby helped Sarah down from the cart, shielded by the trees the two walked to the river which was running swiftly. She bent down to pick certain greyish plants, sweet-smelling: gently, as if not to hurt them. She tied them in a bunch: "It's winter sage," she explained.

"What is it for?"

"For the digestion, catarrh. If you suffer from it, I'll treat you with this."

And with an immaculate smile: "If you rub it on your teeth it makes them whiter."

They sat down on the edge of the water, every so often the sun came out from behind the clouds, and the water became silvery. Hand in hand, for the first time really free and alone. And happy, their difficulties behind them.

Suddenly a squirrel darted out of the trees, it was holding two acorns in its paws. It watched them with its little white-circled eyes: in a few hops it was next to the woman. Barnaby raised his hand as if to frighten it away, but she stopped him. "It has come to greet us," and she stroked the little animal on its head, saying "You should be sleeping in your tree, you should, with this cold."

It seemed to understand, dropped the acorns in her lap, by way of a gift. It then turned around and, rapidly, disappeared among the trees.

Far away a dog could be heard barking. Sir Daniel was not yet to be seen, the sky had turned a sullen grey, a storm threatened, she felt cold.

"Let's go back to the cart," said Barnaby. He offered her his hand to help her rise.

"You know, we still need to know each other properly," said Sarah as they started walking.

"In the biblical sense?" he joked.

"How silly you are!"

They were both remembering, she blushed at the thought — what had happened months before when he had escorted her in the royal forest of Epping to gather herbs for the ointments for the king. It was a night in July, there was the moon, they had tied their horses to a tree. All of a sudden clouds had covered the moon, complete darkness, the cry of the night birds, rustles of animals in the undergrowth, the abrupt passing of a weasel: she had clutched him tightly, and, without a word, screened by the branches of a large willow tree, they had made love.

As they were walking he slipped an arm around her waist, she leaned on his shoulder. She said: "Tell me about your family. My father you've met, and I've told you about my mother."

"You'll soon see my sister, she'll be in Ireland, Daniel will bring her to us. She's good, intelligent. As for your father, how did things go with him?"

"It was as if we had met for the first time," and she told him about that last night.

"Don't worry, Daniel will act as messenger with him too. Perhaps one day he will join us where we are."

"You spoke about Kildare."

"In Ireland we shall be protected, two Catholics that are fleeing Henry's England. We shall find housing in St Bridget's. Can you imagine it? An old Celtic cross beside a fountain in a market-place, a thatched cottage, walls white amidst the green of the meadows."

She recalled the dream one night in Bedlam: a white cottage, the sound of waves on the rocks, Barnaby and a child by the fire. And someone they didn't know, a stranger, at the door. She shivered.

"Weapons that kill."

Carlisle Castle, 24 March 1542

They left the wood.

"Here in the fortress I have friends: we'll meet Fergus – Sir Fergus O'Neill of Leinster. And Donngal, Sir Donngal O'Donnell of Connacht. We were infants together," said Barnaby.

"Tell me."

"I had two brothers, younger than me, Oren and Maurice. Fergus had three: Éogan, Fland and Bran. Donngal had only a sister, Alienor. She had flaxen hair and blue eyes.

"Were you in love with her?"

"So you're jealous!"

He leant to kiss her: "Nothing like that, I was very sensible. I went boating with them on the river, we dived, we played games on each other. Once Alienor hid my clothes. I couldn't leave the water naked, with Alienor there, so I spent hours in it with my teeth chattering."

He added: "Fergus and Donngal, and all the other friends: what a welcome they will give you, I'm longing for you to meet them."

They returned to the cart. At midday that they ate Margery's gingerbread and drank some beer. They refrained from lighting a fire, Sir Daniel had forbidden it. They slept for a while.

"It's getting dark. Barnaby, why doesn't Daniel return?"

"Perhaps his lord is elsewhere. In any case, he has forbidden us to enter the city."

But immediately he thought: "To stay here, outside the walls, at night, with a woman, and the Scots close at hand." He recalled the horrors of Berwick: the fires, the rapes, the massacres. "If Daniel doesn't come, we'll ask for sanctuary in the castle."

He read uncertainty in her eyes. "Better than staying here," he sought to reassure her.

Dusk came. They left the wood, in the lightly falling rain, crossing the green that led to the castle. They were holding each others' hands, he was carrying aloft a lantern. As they reached the moat, the storm broke out: sudden, violent. Barnaby supported Sarah against the gusts of wind, but the lantern was blown to and fro and went out. "Don't be afraid," he told her, "We're almost there."

Then a flash of lightning lighted the darkness and they glimpsed the moat only a few feet away, the drawbridge and the archers on the battlements. They heard someone shouting, saw the archers' bows bent back. They realized the danger: they would be mistaken for the enemy.

"Throw yourself on the ground," shouted Barnaby, and jumped in front of her, arms outspread.

"No, my love, no!" she cried out, and tried to hold him back.

For both of them it was as if their whole life flashed before them in that moment: they would have liked to exchange a thousand thoughts which there had not been time to share

– it had all happened so quickly. She felt ashamed at times, a married woman who had surrendered to him with such willingness: and if one day he should fling it in her face? But then she would tell him of her loneliness, of her desperation at that time. And that other terrible nightmare, the dagger that she had seen on his belt and that had been found at Matthew's side. And despite this, she had not come to love him less. Was this wrong?

And Barnaby: he too would ease his conscience: how else could he look her in the eyes, all life long, while not telling her of the terrible events of that night?

At the same time, in the flashes of lightning, the soldiers on the battlements noticed two figures running forward, bent under their cloaks. They raised the alarm, pulled back their bows, shouted at them to stop – in the din of the storm the two did not hear.

Nor did the commander, Sir William Gibbs, a friend of Barnaby's, hear the cries for help. "Scottish spies, the rebel advance guard. Stop them!" he ordered. The archers loosed a shower of arrows into the darkness.

Sir Daniel arrived back at the wood in the midst of a strong gale. He did not find them in the cart – there was no sign of struggle, everything was in order. He searched for them in the trees, at the river. Might they have gone into town? But he had just come from there and had not seen them. In the castle, perhaps? He remembered that Barnaby had friends there, he felt a cold shiver go down his spine, like a bolt of lightning there came to mind the words of the old seer: 'Beware of your friends, they have weapons that can kill'.

He jumped back on his horse and spurred it in a desperate rush towards the fortress.

The rain had stopped, the trees were soaking wet, and still. The moon shone clearly on the castle walls, the mound, the band of silver that was the river. Silence, peace.

When he arrived at the moat, Sir Daniel saw the light of many torches and a group of soldiers standing in a circle around something on the ground: he made himself known to them, and approached.

On the ground were two bodies, wrapped in cloaks bespattered with blood and mud. He leant over the nearest, saw the gentle face of a young man now lifeless.

Leaned over him was a woman, beautiful, dressed as a boy, her hair which had slipped down from under her bonnet, long, dark. She was stroking his face, murmuring soft words, the shadow of a desperate smile on her lips, and a hand on her unborn child, as if to shield it.

Epilogue

Sarah: On the death of his friend Sir Barnaby, Sir Daniel took her into his own family, where she was lovingly cared for; in the meantime he went to Ireland to give the news of his death to Barnaby's family. After that he accompanied Sarah back to London, and entrusted her to his father.

It was Sir Daniel who brought news of Sir Barnaby's death to Sir Robert and to Sarah's father. So Sarah returned to her father's house and they lived together during his final years, consoled by the presence of an enchanting child, Leah.

For **Sir Robert** the sovereign's demise, five years after the events narrated, was release from a nightmare. Finally freed from the king's rancour, he returned to Cambridge with his wife Constance, and there enjoyed many peaceful years. As did the rest of the family, the good Margery and Philip. And when the latter married and had children, Sir Robert's house was filled with the sounds of play and laughter, as Lady Constance had always dreamed.

King Henry died in January 1547, in the meantime he had married for the sixth and last time. The woman, Lady Katherine Parr, a nobleman's widow, cultured and wealthy, proved to be an excellent queen and survived him.

Sir Thomas Howard third Duke of Norfolk, uncle of the beheaded Anne Boleyn and Kathryn Howard, after a brief spell in the Tower and a life of wickedness, intrigue and abuse, returned to his lands in Norfolk, where he died peacefully in his bed.

Sir Nicholas Sherman continued over the years to serve King Henry and the Duke of Norfolk. At the sovereign's death he passed into the service of Henry's son, Edward VI. But when the young king died and his sister Mary – 'Bloody Mary' – , succeeded to the throne, there were plots on the part of the jealous Spanish courtiers. Fearing for his life, Nicholas fled to Ireland. When Mary died he came back to England and retired to his estate in Cambridge.

For those who wish to know more

Ackroyd, Peter, *London. The Biography*. Chatto & Windus, London **2000**

Al-Dabbagh SA., *Ibn Al-Nafis and the Pulmonary Circulation,* The Lancet, Volume 311, Issue 8074, Page 1148, **27 May 1978**

Alsop, J.D., *Innovation in Tudor Taxation,* English Historical Review, 99 (**1984**), 83-93
The Structure of Early Tudor Finance, c.1509-1558, in C. Coleman and D. R. Starkey (eds.), *Revolution Reassessed,* pp. 135-62

Andrews, K.R., *Trade, Plunder and Settlement: Maritime Enterprise and the Genesis of the British Empire, 1480-1630,* Cambridge, **1984**

Anglo, S., *Spectacle, Pageantry, and Early Tudor Policy,* Oxford, **1969**

Baskerville, Geoffrey, *English Monks and the Suppression of the Monasteries,* Yale University Press, New Haven, N.J., **1937**

Bernard, G. W., *The Pardon of the Clergy Reconsidered,* Journal of Ecclesiastical History, 37 (**1986**), 258-82

Brewer, J.S., Gairdner, James and Brodie, R.H. , eds., *Letters and Papers, Foreign and Domestic, in the Reign of Henry VIII,* H.M.S.O., London **1864- 1910**

Brigden, S. E., *Popular Disturbance and the Fall of Thomas Cromwell and the Reformers, 1539-1540,* Historical Journal, 24 (**1981**), 257-8

Chambers, D. S., *Cardinal Wolsey and the Papal Tiara,* Bulletin of the Institute of Historical Research, 38 (**1965**), 20-30

Cooper, J. P., *Henry VII's Last Years Reconsidered,* Historical Journal, 2 (**1959**), 103-29

Cornwall, J., *English Population in the Early Sixteenth Century,* Economic History Review, 2nd series, 23 (**1970**), 32-44)

Cressy, David, *Birth, Marriage and Death: Ritual Religions and the Life-Cycle in Tudor and Stuart England,* Oxford University Press, Oxford **1977**
Levels of Illiteracy in England, 1530-1730, Historical Journal, 20 (**1977**). 1-23
Spectacle and Power: Apollo and Solomon at the Court of Henry VIII, History Today, 32 (Oct. **1982**), 16-22

Crombie, A. C. , *Da S. Agostino a Galileo, Storia della scienza dal V al XVII secolo,* Giangiacomo Feltrinelli Editore, Milano **1970**

Darby, Henry Clifford, *A New Historical Geography of England before 1600,* Cambridge University Press, Cambridge **1976**

Dickens. A.G., *Secular and Religious Motivation in the Pilgrimage of Grace,* in G. J. Cumming (editor), *Studies in Church History,* IV, *The Province of York, 1509-1558* (Leiden **1968),** 39-54)

Doner, Margaret, *Lies and Lust in the Tudor Court, The Fifth Wife of Henry VIII,* iUniverse, Inc., New York - Lincoln - Shanghai, **2004**

Ellis, S. G., Crown, *Community and Government in the English territories, 1450- 1575,* History, 71 (1966). 187-204
England in the Tudor State, Historical Journal, 26 (**1983**), 201-12

Elton, G. R. , *The Tudor Constitution: Documents and Commentary,* Cambridge University Press, Cambridge, **1960**
Mid Tudor Finance, Historical Journal, 20 (1977), 737-40

Erickson, Carolly, *Il grande Harry,* Arnoldo Mondadori Editore, Milano **1980/2002**

Fines, J, *Heresy and Trials in the Dioceses of Coventry and Lichfield, 1511-12,* Journal of Ecclesiastical History, 14 (**1963**), 160-74

Fisher, F.J, *Influenza and Inflation in Tudor England,* Economic History Review, 2nd series, 18 (**1965**), 120-9

Fletcher, Anthony, *Tudor Rebellions,* Longman, London **1968**

Fraser, Antonia, *The Six Wives of Henry VIII,* George Weidenfeld & Nicolson Ltd, **1992;** Phoenix Press Orion Books Ltd, Orion House 5 Upper St Martin's Lane, London WC2H 9EA, **2002.**

Frugoni, Arsenio e Chiara, *Storia di un giorno in una Città Medievale,* Editori Laterza, Roma – Bari, **2002**

Grace, F.R., *The Life and Career of Thomas Howard, Third Duke of Norfolk,* unpublished Nottingham MA dissertation **(1961)**

George, Margaret, *The Autobiography of Henry VIII,* St Martin's Press, 175 Fifth Avenue, New York, N.Y: 10010, **1986.**

Guy, John, *Tudor England,* Oxford University Press, London **1988**
Henry VIII and the 'Praemunire? Manoeuvres of 1530-1531, English Historical Review, 97 **(1982),** 481-503
Law, Faction and Parliament in the Sixteenth Century, Historical Journal, 28 **(1985),** 441-53
Law, Lawyers, and the English Reformation, History Today, 35 **(November 1985)** 16-22

Hall, Edward, *Chronicle Containing the History of England,* J. Johnson, London **1809**

Hanson, Marilee, *Tudor England, 1485-1603,* "*Letters of the Six Wives of Henry VIII*" (download: http://englishhistory.net/tudor.html)

Harriss, G. L., *Thomas Cromwell's New Principle of Taxation,* English Historical Review, 93 (**1978**) 721-38

Herbert, Edward, 1st Baron of Cherbury, *The Life and Reign of King Henry VIII,* Andrew Clark, London **1672**

Hoak, D. E., *The Secret History of the Tudor Court: The King's Coffers and the King's Purse, 1542-1553,* Journal of British Studies, 26 (**1987**) 208-31

Ilardi, Vincent, *Renaissance Vision from Spectacles to Telescopes,* American Philosophical Society, Philadelphia, **2007**

Lindsey, Karen, *Divorced, Beheaded, Survived,* Da Capo Press, Cambridge, Massachusetts, **1995**

Miller, H., Henry *VIII's Unwritten Will: Grants of Lands and Honours in 1547,* in E. W. Ives, R.J. Knecht and J.J Scarisbrick (editors), Wealth and Power in Tudor England (**London 1978**), 87-105
London and Parliament in the Reign of Henry VIII, Bulletin of the Institute of Historical Research, 35 (**1962**), 128-49

Martin, Rhona, *Writing Historical Fiction,* A & C Black, London, 1988

Moberly, Charles Edward, *Henry VIII King of England, 1491-1547,* C.Scribner's Sons, **1906**
Mumby, Frank Arthur, *The Youth of Henry VIII, A Narrative in Contemporary Letters,* Houghton Miffling Company, Boston & New York, **1913**

Plowden, Alison, *Tudor Women, Queens & Commoners,* **1979** Weidenfield & Nicolson; **2007** Sutton Publishing Ltd, Stroud, Gloucestershire

Pollard, Albert Frederick, *Henry VIII,* Longmans Green & Co., London **1905/1951**

Redworth, G., *A Study in the Formulation of Policy: The Genesis and Evolution of the Act of Six Articles,* Journal of Ecclesiastical History, 37 (**1986**), 42-67

Ridgway, Claire, *The Fall of Anne Boleyn, A Countdown,* **2012**;
The Real Truth about the Tudors, The Anne Boleyn Collection, **2012**;
Sweating Sickness in a Nutshell, **2014**;
Tudor Places of Great Britain, **2015**;
On This Day in Tudor History, **2015**.
Made Global Publishing, both Paperback and Kindle Editions.

Sansom, C.J. , *Dark Fire,* Penguin Group, 80 Strand, London, **2004**
Dissolution, A Novel of Tudor England, Penguin Group, 80 Strand, London **2003**
Sovereign, Macmillan **2006**, poi Pan Macmillan, London **2007 – 2008**

Scarisbrick, J. J., *Wealth and Power in Tudor England: Essays,* with E.W. Ives, R. J. Knecht, J.J., Bindoff, T. Stanley. Athlone Press **1978**
The Pardon of the Clergy, 1531, Cambridge Historical Journal, 12 (**1956**), 22-39

St Clare Byrne, Muriel, editor, *The Lisle Letters,* Penguin Books, Harmondsworth, Middlesex, England, **1983**

Stow, John, *A Survey of London,* London **1598**. Reissued by Sutton Publishing, Stroud, Glos., 1997

Warnicke, R.M., *Sexual Heresy at the Court of Henry VIII,* Historical Journal, 30, (**1987**), 247-68

Weir, Alison, *The Six Wives of Henry VIII,* The Bodley Head **1991**; Pimlico Edition **1992**; Vintage, Random House, 20 Vauxhall Bridge Road, London SW1V 2SA, **2007**

Whiting, R., *Abominable Idols: Images and Image Breaking under Henry VIII,* Journal of Ecclesiastical History, 33 (**1982**), 30-47

Williams, Neville, *Henry VIII and His Court,* Macmillan, New York **1971**

Wilson, Derek, *In the Lion's Court: Power, Ambition, and Sudden Death in the Reign of Henry VIII,* St Martin's Press, New York **2002**

Wriothesley, Charles, *A Chronicle of England during the Reigns of the Tudors,* from 1485 to 1559, Camden Society, 1885 / Kessinger Publishing Rare Reprints 2007

Acknowledgements

We would like to thank Laura Lepri and Bruna Miorelli for their rigorous yet supportive editing, and Lucia Incerti Caselli, Silvia Cutaia, Maria Di Donato, Anna Fassini, Christian Hill, Serena and Domenico Lazzaro, Gabriella Mariano, Chiara Motton, Silvia Penati, Paola Pirzio and Mary Shannon for reviewing the manuscript and for their suggestions.

We are also grateful to all the authors mentioned in the bibliography, and particularly to Peter Ackroyd, Antonia Fraser, Margaret George, Philippa Gregory, Karen Lindsey, Liza Picard, Alison Plowden, Albert Frederick Pollard, C.J.Sansom and Alison Weir.

For their guidance, we thank again Laura Lepri, Bruna Miorelli, John Gardner, Rhona Martin, Owain Sowden and Sol Stein.

About the authors

After completing her studies in Italy and the UK, and after teaching English for several years, **Mariella Moretti** moved to work in the field of applied linguistics. For a number of years she worked in educational publishing, and is currently engaged in the writing historical fiction, and in the research and study that this involves.

After many years as a teacher of English, in a variety of fields, roles and locations, **Colin Sowden** now works as a free-lance examiner, translator and teacher-trainer, with a special interest in course design, materials creation and writing.

Printed by Amazon Italia Logistica S.r.l.
Torrazza Piemonte (TO), Italy

38206227R00143